The absence of sound woke me up. I'd been hearing Nick's labored breaths in my subconscious for hours. I knew he was going to die, but sleep let me take the coward's way out. If I slept, he would be fine in my dreams; he would still be there when I woke up.

Moving like an old lady, I pushed out of the chair. In tiny steps, I walked toward the cot. Halfway there and the blast of the gunshot pierced the quiet dawn, shattering it like glass. Nick's body was hidden by the broad shoulders of the man wielding the gun. A sob broke out. I tried to stop it but the tears poured down my face as I rushed to Seth.

I pounded my fists against his back. Incoherent words flew from my lips. The gun fell with a metallic clang and I found myself wrapped in warm, solid male. The last place I wanted to be—in the arms of Nick's executioner. This man who'd taken my responsibility as his own.

Other books by Jill James

LOVE IN THE TIME OF ZOMBIES

JILL JAMES

 Gray Sweater Press

Love in the Time of Zombies
Time of Zombies, Book 1
All Rights Reserved.
Copyright 2015 Jill James
Poems attributed to Seth Ripley in this manuscript are
© Jill James
ISBN# 978-0692376638
Cover Art © Elaina Lee at For The Muse Designs
All rights reserved – Used with permission

Gray Sweater Press
www.graysweaterpress.com

DEDICATION

This book is dedicated to Max Brooks and Jonathan Maberry for inspiring me with the best zombies books out there.

To Carrie Ryan, Dana Fredsti, Rhiannon Frater, Mira Grant, and Bonnie Dee for showing me women can write zombies too. Thank you, ladies.

IN THE BEGINNING...

I could start by quoting the old saying about good intentions and the road to hell. But what is done is done and the human race doesn't get a do-over. We all have to live with the consequences of our actions. Or in this case, live with the actions of our government.

I could start by saying I miss my husband, but that would be as big a lie as the one we were told would save countless millions and instead killed them—sort of. I'm sure the president meant well. I'm sure in his grief over his son's death by influenza, along with one-hundred million other people in the United States it seemed like a great plan to add a new flu vaccine to our food and water supply to save those of us left. Riots rocked the major cities. The anti-vaccination people tried to take on the government. The government won. What a shock.

It took an executive order, but President Andrew Thomas got his wish. I'm sure a scientist somewhere knew the risks of mutation and didn't speak up. Or maybe, they didn't get the chance to say anything. Events unfolded pretty damned quick once the spraying was completed. The infected attacked as soon as they turned and the dead didn't stay dead.

I could start by saying that life now sucked, but at what time in human history haven't we thought life sucked and the apocalypse was just around the corner? It's kind of like paranoid people. Sometimes there *is* someone out to get you. Sometimes the apocalypse really *is* right around the corner.

I could give you the step-by-step events that led to our downfall and the almost extinction of the human race, but it's been told many times before in books and movies and it pretty much happened just as they said it would.

Or I could tell you my name is Emily Gray and this is the story of my life in the time of zombies.

CHAPTER ONE

Guess you never know. Who would have thought something as terrible as the zombie apocalypse would bring me something as wonderful as Seth Ripley?

Of course, the zombies got my mother and my father, and my husband, Carl. Pretty much, they got my whole family. Okay, my husband Carl had been an asshole so he was no great loss. Never could keep it in his pants, if I may be so crude. If he could've kept it in his pants, he may have kept that appendage altogether. But, it was the early days of the Z virus mutation and how could he know the hooker he took to the cheap by-the-hour motel had the sickness? I'm sure he didn't realize anything until the woman chewed it off, to be honestly blunt. He never was a great one for paying attention during sex as it was. Oh, maybe in the early days of our marriage, but he'd changed in the last few years, just before the end of the world.

Five years of him spreading it far and wide

to prove his virility and all I was left with was a one-sheet police report and a blurred photo of Carl with one between the opaque, dead eyes. The police had stopped trying to take sickies to the hospital a couple of weeks before. By the time Carl was attacked it was kill 'em, identify 'em, and burn 'em in a pile. KIB was the order of the day. A few weeks after that and they skipped the identify part of the acronym too. A few weeks more and there weren't enough police or bullets for the killing part either.

Six months had passed and the police were all gone, along with the military. Now it was survival of the fittest. Never in a million years would I have pictured myself—neglected, society trophy-wife, Emily Gray, in that category. Guess you never know.

Your day could start so shitty and end so... well, not great, because there weren't too many great days anymore. The only definition to divide the monotony of the days were get bitten by a zombie day and not get bitten by a zombie day. But that day would turn out better than most. At least it would with a great deal of hindsight and distance from the event. Adding a whole hell of a lot of seeing a silver-lining after the fact helped too.

As with most days, I had zombie patrol for the morning, which was so not my best time of the day. But zombies don't have an off switch so we had to hunt first thing in the morning to clear the perimeter around the giant mall.

Did you know shopping centers are the best

defense against zombies? Me neither, until I got shipped out of what was left of San Francisco to the middle of nowhere—Brentwood. I'd never even heard of the town before I got sent there. Shopping centers are like medieval castles. Brick up the front doors and small back doors and the roof is like the battlements of a castle. Zombies can't climb. Thank God for any small favor we could get. It's about the only advantage we have. Because we have to sleep and the zombies don't.

We were the last escapees of the city by the bay. Pre-Z the city had a population of more than 850, 000. In the end, San Francisco had 5,000 living beings to round up and ship to other communities to the east. The lieutenant governor (the governor had turned on live television and been put down) declared San Francisco the land of the undead, and blew up the bridges connecting it to the rest of the state and collapsed the Caldecott Tunnel for good measure. A bunch of massive explosions of entire city blocks to the south and San Francisco was pretty much an island of zombies.

My skin had burned lobster-red my first week of roof living here. San Francisco is more known for fog and chilly days than for getting a suntan. Once I tanned, it was the burnished copper of my ancestors—Native Americans of some unknown tribe, according to my mother. Way back in our ancestry, she had always been sure to add. The long hair my husband had insisted on was gone—happily. Long hair and zombies did not mix. My first day there I'd seen a young, blonde girl pulled back by her long braid and devoured in a dirt field. Long hair gone. Also happily gone, the extra thirty pounds I had carried through my unhappy marriage years. Running from zombies was the best aerobic exercise around. The penalty for missing a day of exercise was death—or nondeath in our case.

No one knew for sure back then if the animals were susceptible to the mutation, and what eating them would do to us, so breakfast was lots of fruits, vegetables, and soy patties. After six months of eating the food and drinking the water, either we were going to turn undead or not as far as I was concerned. I looked at it like this, if we were going to turn, we would have already done so. Scientific types were still testing cows and pigs to see if they just had the flu vaccine in them or if it would mutate in them too. Hadn't seen any pigs or cows running amok yet.

Fruits, veggies, and soy weren't too bad, considering in my last days in the city some of the inhabitants had been considering eating the grass in their yards. Cats and dogs had been missing from the streets and the rat population had been way down.

Brentwood, and the surrounding small towns, was a farmer's market dream. Orchards for miles around and farms galore. With the population down to one or two thousand, there was plenty for everyone.

Food wasn't a big problem. Harvesting and transporting it was. It's hard to pick a row of corn if you're afraid the man-eating undead are in the next row over. I'd never been the growing type. If it needed care and tending, I would probably kill it. Fortunately, I was an excellent shooter. Who knew? I'd never shot a gun in my life before. Why would I? San Francisco was the land of anti-gun belief. Maybe if we'd had more gun-toting citizens we might have held the city.

When we got there, they'd put us through a bunch of tests: agility, strength, skills, and shooting. I'd scored a hundred at all distances. No picking apples for this girl, I was a member of the undead hunting patrol.

Breakfast out of the way, I cleaned up my section of the roof. Gathering up my dirty clothes, and believe me, you haven't seen dirty until you try to get zombie guts out of your shirt, I took them to my friend, Michelle, who had laundry duty this month. Michelle Greggs had been on the wild ride with me out of San Francisco. We'd clung to each other all night as the horde of undead tried to get to the fresh meat inside the fortified school bus. Rotted fingers poked between the welded metal sheets and their moans stayed with us long after the trip was over. We'd been friends ever since. Shit like that is a real bonding moment.

She stopped me with an upraised hand, and then grabbed a pair of surgical gloves before taking my clothes. We'd all told her countless times that she couldn't get the mutated virus from simple contact; we pretty much all had the virus, but she continued to use the gloves. We all have our idiosyncrasies since this all started and we'd let her have hers.

She dropped into a curtsy. "And would madam like these pressed and folded as well?"

I played along. "Yes and any spots left will come out of your pay." I put up my chin and looked down my nose at her. I could have done a dowager countess proud.

Michelle laughed. I would play any silly game to get that light, airy sound from her, even if it were a mockery of my pre-Z life. Or maybe, my pre-Z life had been a mockery of reality all along.

Unlike me, my friend had loved her husband with all her heart and had to kill him when he'd turned. She'd told me the sad story on the bus with the caveat that she would never mention it again.

"Now, go kill those skinbags," she ordered.

"Yes, ma'am," I replied, giving her a snappy salute. We all had our names for the zombies we had to kill. Some used other names to make it easier. Parents in our group used funny names to make it less scary for the children. Way back when, before my time, there had been a late-night local show; Creature Features, and the parents had taken to calling the zombies Black Lagooners. But for the life of me, I couldn't see how anything made what we were going through less scary. Maybe kids had a defense mechanism I was missing. I was scared shitless most days.

I left my friend with a smile on her face, so that took some of the crappiness out of the day.

Grabbing my canteen, I headed to the weapons cache to get mine. Standing by the pile was my partner for the day, Nick Cruz. He was only sixteen, but his kill rank was two times mine and it showed in his eyes. They didn't belong on a kid. He was built like a linebacker, which he'd been before the feces hit the proverbial fan. I liked the days I was teamed up with Nick, which was most days. We worked well together. He was a local and he'd tell me stories of Brentwood in its finer days.

I greeted him and we bumped fists. He handed me my crossbow and a rifle. I slung the crossbow on my back and grabbed a holder for the bolts. The rifle had a solid weight in my hands. I never knew what kind I'd get each day, not that it mattered because I can't tell the difference anyway. After six months, you'd think I would know all about weapons, but the letters and numbers of the gun model just flew right out of my brain. Hand me a gun, hand me the bullets, I'm good to go. I could field-strip and clean them with my eyes shut, so I guess that's something more useful than being able to plan a cotillion for five hundred; a seating chart and all.

We went out in a group of eight. A team of two people went each direction on the map. North, South, East, and West. Nick and I got south for the day. It's my favorite. We could walk straight down the old bypass with Mount Diablo on our right. The view is breathtaking. For the first few miles, the cars have been cleared and you could see for a good distance. Last week, a fire whipped through the hills around us, so the stubble is short, burned, with nowhere to hide. This is a good thing, although the burning smell and drifting smoke lasted for a while.

The pop of gunfire started as the spotters on the corners took out the undead outside the perimeter of the mall. Nick and I checked out the area when the popping stopped. Spotting no one, dead or alive, we shimmied down the rope ladder that would be pulled up as soon as we were clear. I'd been doing this for months now and my heart still stopped beating when we jumped down and the ladder was pulled up. An even scarier moment for me than meeting the Queen of England, and trying to remember not to touch her, unless she touched you first. Believe you me that had been scary.

I stood by the cargo containers stacked to make temporary walls on what was the road into the interior of the shopping center. Putting the binoculars up to my eyes, I turned in a semicircle to scope out the area. The teams from the shopping center across the road were starting their morning too. The faint pop-pop-pop of rifles carried across the empty space.

Once Nick was down, I tried to look elsewhere as the ladder was pulled up. I closed my eyes and clutched my lucky necklace in my fist. The metal edge bit into my palm and reassured me by its very existence. The necklace was a thirteenth birthday present from my parents. The center was a fifty-cent piece minted in my birth year, inserted into a fancy, silver filigree setting. It never came off my body. I slept and showered with it.

We trekked across a field to the broken asphalt of the Highway 4 Bypass. The first time we'd gone this way, Nick had told me of the grand plans and tax dollars used for a new road, but the economy not only didn't bounce back from the recession, it sunk into an abyss that made the former Great Depression look like a temporary dip in the Dow Jones Index. I'd been oblivious in San Francisco. Carl came from money and I guess the city was better off to start with than the outlying East Bay. The zombie apocalypse was a great equalizer. It did what Occupy Wall Street couldn't. Money was worthless and your skills put food on the table, clothes on your back, and a canvas roof, at least, over your head. Or not, if your skills sucked or were no longer useful. Not much call these days for bankers and lawyers, maybe there never would be again.

At the Bypass, we headed south and another team headed north toward the next town over— Antioch. I waved at Robert Jones and Joseph Jones, the other team heading that way. Bob and Joe were partners in every way. I couldn't imagine seeing one without the other. Another way the virus equalized our world. Bob and Joe were married the first chance they got. With everything going on and same-sex marriage on-again and off-again, they hadn't found the time. When the dead could walk, most of your stupid beliefs went right out the window. We had several gay/lesbian couples, even some threesomes, and foursomes. Whatever worked to make a family unit with adults and the numerous orphans left from the virus. Whatever! I'm staying happily single. After Carl, I'm in no freaking hurry to be hitched to another person anytime soon. If ever. Thanks to my skills, for the first time in my life, I could take care of myself. I would never rely on a man again.

Nick's whisper brought me out of my thoughts as our boots plodded on the road, the echoes bouncing back in the silence, "Joe and Bob saw some undead this way yesterday, so be on the lookout."

I gasped. "There haven't been any for a week. Not since the fire burned out. Where do you think they came from?"

"There're a couple of schools down Balfour. Joe said some of them appeared to be kids. I hate undead kids. Last time we ran across some, I had to take out ones I used to know."

I put my hand on his shoulder. "Let's go the other way. We can hit that little shopping center with the Safeway. I heard they are growing tomatoes."

"I could die for a tomato," I joked.

"But you would come back as the undead and I'd have to shoot you in the head," he replied.

I groaned at the latest, sick, zombie humor going around between the teens at the compound, but Nick smiled.

CHAPTER TWO

The darkness of her eyes held the terror of the day.
The golden of her skin glistened with crimson rivers.
She wore the patina of lost ones like vagabond rags
draped on her bowed, weighted shoulders.
— Seth Ripley

The zombie apocalypse could end any fucking time as far as Seth Ripley was concerned. Six months had dragged on like years. When he envisioned actual years of this he was ready to swallow his S & W 1911 to end the pain. The only thing stopping him was God and the virus. Also, the thought of his mother's pain at the idea they wouldn't be together in Heaven someday. Catholic guilt will get you every time. He slapped the steering wheel, cursed, and then crossed himself.

Running supplies and messages between communities at least let him think he had a purpose, a reason for remaining on this forsaken land formerly known as the great state of California. Before the Z virus, he'd just been a truck driver. He'd taken loads from point A to point B, paid the mortgage on a house that was so far underwater he would have to pay the bank to take it back, and lived paycheck to paycheck to buy things he thought he needed. Now, he traveled from enclave to enclave, bringing messages from loved ones, needed goods, and getting paid with food, supplies, and sometimes a bed other than the one in his truck.

Coming from Antioch, he sped down the cleared Bypass Road, glad, yet again, that the people at the Streets of Brentwood group had moved the cars off into the grass months ago. His gaze swept the weed-infested, cracked asphalt, on the lookout for the undead. He swerved to miss one dragging its useless limbs across the road. Crossing himself, he uttered a prayer for the lost soul just as a shot rang out and the man collapsed onto the pavement.

He slowed the truck and pulled up beside two men. Stopping, he saw Joseph and Robert from the Streets of Brentwood. Seth rolled down his window and waved at the men, shouting a hello.

The pair rolled the dead man into the grass, spray painted an X on the road, and then radioed their location to base. He knew a clean-up crew would come out later and incinerate the now truly dead.

He leaned out the window. "How's it going?

"Not too bad," they replied in unison, as usual. It was either that or they completed each other's sentences.

"Didn't see you guys last time I was through here."

"We've been sweeping south and west lately. Some skinbags that way lately," Bob replied.

"Nick and Emily have south today and they radioed in that they are going southeast to the Safeway group," Joe added.

"You guys are gonna have to clear out the schools one day. They're already partway fenced and protected. Wouldn't take much to clear them out and have a small community with space and grounds to plant?"

"Yeah, just kill some kids," Bob said, looking at the ground.

"Undead kids," Joe finished.

Joe looked up. "What are you bringing today? Please say something other than tofu and veggie burgers."

"I've got a load of fish today. The ham radio network passed the word from the scientific group Lawrence Livermore Lab. Fish and chicken are now on the safe list. Just have the flu vaccine, not the mutated Z."

"Yes," the guys cried in unison and bumped fists.

"So, who is this Emily?"

Joe replied while Bob swept the area, gun at the ready. "You must have missed her. She came with a group from the city, the last one. Been here a few months, but she does patrol. I swear that girl could shoot the wings off a fly."

Bob turned around from his surveying. "Cute little thing. I would totally tap that if I were straight. Dark hair, dark eyes, sun-kissed skin, and with meat in all the right places, if you know what I mean."

Seth's mind went down roads it hadn't traveled in a long while. Visions of an Amazon warrior princess filled his head. He'd had his share of women before the apocalypse, even a failed engagement with both parties okay with the breakup, but nothing since this mess all started. It's hard to fight zombies and find time to have a relationship, when you didn't know if there would be a tomorrow. Even when you tried to keep a glimmer of hope alive.

"Gonna head on in. Give you guys a lift?"

They shook their heads. "Nope, just heading out. Heard the Target group got a bunch of fabric and can make anything you want. Been seeing a few deaders too, so we'll do some clearing."

"I'm staying over tonight, so see you at the fish fry."

"I'm not missing that," they replied in unison.

Seth rolled up the truck window as the men started down the road, going north. He crossed himself and said a prayer for their safety.

Driving down the road, he turned in to the Streets of Brentwood. He stopped beside what had been REI and Ulta at one time. The sporting goods store had been cleaned out to the studs. The bikes, tents, and sleeping bags put to good use. The beauty store had been cleared as well for barter goods with other communities. The doors and windows were gone, making them hard for anyone, zombie or live person, to hide.

Seth hit his horn twice, paused, and hit it once more. The signal was out of courtesy, he'd been spotted long before he stopped in front of the container gate. The CB radio squawked at him. He picked up the receiver.

"Who is the president of the United States of America?"

Not that zombies seemed able to drive; yet, but they sure as hell couldn't talk. Moans and groans didn't count.

"President Andrew Thomas."

"Welcome to the Streets of Brentwood."

In a feat of mechanics he hadn't quite figured out yet, the containers lifted from the ground via two cranes on the roofs of the buildings on either side of the street. Once it was high enough, he drove through. In his side view mirror, he watched as the containers slowly settled back down to the ground with a groan and a solid thump of security.

The road inside looped around in an oval with the stores on the outside and water features and gardens in the middle. He drove slowly toward the movie theatre on the lookout for kids who seemed to be everywhere. Tension left him as his shoulders sagged and he breathed deeply. Something about little kids just let you believe there was a future, maybe. There was a comforting sense of security here.

With a hiss of hydraulics, he braked in front of the theatre. At one time, it had been state of the art. Now it was the group's warehouse and showed movies once a week as long as the wind turbines continued getting power out on Vasco Road and funneled it to the shopping center. The theatre had been pretty much all computer-run and the stockpile of movies remained.

Seth cut the motor and hopped down from the truck. A group of men were converging on the back of the trailer to help him unload. A solidly-built man walked toward him. Jack Canida was a walking poster for Army Strong. He'd been an army captain on leave at the time the shit went down. Jack was a natural-born leader. People flocked to him and with a show of hands elected him commander of The Streets of Brentwood. Within days, he had the location fortified, cleared of the undead, and supplied with weapons, ammo, and food.

They shook hands. Seth looked into a face that he wouldn't have wanted to confront in a dark alley. Jack had changed over the past few months. The first time he'd brought food, and news of the outside world, the man had been outgoing and talkative, sure that things would right themselves swiftly once the army arrived. Two weeks later the army arrived, complimented him on a job well done, officially promoted him to colonel and commander of the mall base, and left him with explosives and the suggestion to demo the restaurants out front and the parking lots to have ground for crops. Not exactly a forecast of things being back to normal anytime soon.

That was the last Canida or The Streets of Brentwood heard of them. The army was gone. The government was gone except for a president who couldn't leave the bunker. They were all on their own. No wonder Jack looked as worn out as he did; he was responsible for 250 souls.

"What do you have for us today, Ripley?"

Seth smiled. "A load of fish. Science guys put it on the safe list, along with chickens."

That put a little happiness on Jack's face. "The people will be happy to hear that. I must get twenty reports a day that veggie burgers aren't cutting it."

"But at least you guys have plenty of fruits and vegetables," Seth added. The smile left his face. The day he'd gotten him and his mother, Carla out of Oakland, the people had been reduced to cats and dogs. The food drops had stopped and the city was declared a total loss. He shuddered. In a town known for violence, they would have fought the gangs for some veggie burgers.

He brought his dark thoughts back to hear Jack ordering the men to unload the truck. He tossed his keys to one of them to unlock the back. The sound of the lock disengaging was followed by the crash of the door being pushed up. A young boy brought back his keys.

"Walk with me," Jack asked.

He knew the commander did a loop of the mall several times a day. He wasn't an Ivory Tower kind of leader. The man knew who was sick, who needed extra rations for a pregnant spouse, or who wasn't eating and giving up. Kids ran up to him and found out the candy supply in his many pockets never ran dry.

They'd walked to the opposite end of the mall, the most vulnerable because it had been the most open. Containers were stacked three high on this end, with men patrolling the top. A set of breakaway stairs led up. They could be pushed over in an extreme emergency.

Seth had just reached the top when a thunderous noise thumped up the stairs. He turned and saw a young teenage girl, out of breath, rushing over to Jack. She skidded to a stop, and put her hands on her knees and panted heavily.

Jack placed a hand on her back and leaned

down. Her news came out in spurts.

"Safeway... Emily and Nick... everyone infected."

"What about Emily and Nick?" Canida barked out.

She stood up. "They used their walkie-talkies. Everyone at the Safeway is dead or undead. N-Nick and Emily are trapped on top of a delivery truck."

He caught the girl's stutter and fast blush. Nick was something more to her than just a member of the Streets group. Taking a deep breath, Seth blurted out, "I'll go. I'll take off the trailer and go in my truck. It's big enough even with just the truck to take out anyone and I'll have room for Nick and this Emily easily."

"Beth, keep this quiet. We don't need a panic yet. Okay?"

She nodded at the commander. "Yes, sir."

"Good," Jack replied and turned to Seth. He pulled his walkie-talkie off of his belt. "John, this is Canida. Double-time on that unload, Ripley needs his truck."

"Okay, you're good to go. Thank you. Grab a walkie-talkie from John before you go."

Seth put his hand on Jack's shoulder. "I'll bring your people back if they're alive and take care of them if they're not."

CHAPTER THREE

The stoplights swung in the rising wind. The wind here was either nonexistent or blowing with a roaring train sound across the open spaces. With the window open, Seth heard the creak of the lights weight on the bouncing poles. Moans echoed from the intersection across from the Safeway shopping center.

"Damn," he cursed, reaching for his rifle in the rear. He'd known the center was a massacre waiting to happen from the first time he'd made a drop-off. The distance between buildings was too wide to enclose. The group settled for all living on the grocery store's roof, with a few cars across the openings. It wasn't enough.

Shots rang out from the paved parking lot as he shifted gears and stepped on the gas. He decided to go in the front. The cars were still moved aside, probably for the delivery truck he spotted in front of the store. Two people stood on top, shooting into the horde below. The store had twenty-five souls the last time he'd been here; today he counted ten. Make that eight as two more shots rang out.

A young boy and girl stood on the roof of a truck trailer. The girl sighted down the rifle and got off two more headshots.

Seth pulled on the air horn. A blast echoed across the empty space, bouncing off the storefronts. Zombies turned and started shuffling toward the truck. He blasted them again with sound. Rolling up his window, he pushed on the trapdoor above his seat and hopped out to the roof of his truck. The kids slid off the roof of their perch, climbed down and jumped to the asphalt.

The sway of her breasts in her thin shirt told him the girl wasn't as much of a kid as he'd first thought. Seth aimed and shot the three in front of him in the leg, shattering kneecaps and taking them to the ground.

"Let's go," he shouted to the pair.

The young woman gave him a withering glare and finished the two in front of her, stopping to cap the three he'd shot.

She marched over to him. So close, he felt her heavy breathing on his chest. Her dark eyes stared into him, black pools of anger. Just in front of him, he saw the lines around her eyes that said this was a full-grown woman, the fluidity of her body, the laugh lines in her face summed up the picture.

"What in the hell is your problem? You have to shoot them in the head." Her body shook and he stood on guard in case she decided not only the zombies needed to be shot in the head today.

"They're incapacitated. They can't get me. It isn't my choice to be judge, jury, and executioner."

Her mouth dropped open. "You are shitting me, right? You can't be that stupid. A living zombie is a dangerous zombie. They're dead; I'm just finishing the job."

He put a hand on her shoulder, which she promptly shook off. "What is dead? They are walking, talking, eating. Even if by chance they are dead, they've lost their souls. I'm not going to be responsible for sending them to Hell unless I absolutely have to."

Her response was cut off by the boy's scream.

They turned to see the last zombie biting the kid on his arm. Before Seth could think, the girl had the gun up and shooting. The undead guy had a hole between his eyes and fell to the ground, taking the kid with him.

Seth brought his gun up and scanned the area. No sounds, no movement. Except for the rising whip of the wind, there was deafening silence. He squatted and checked beneath the two trucks. Nothing.

He hopped up and ran with the young woman to the kid's side. He gasped. It was Nick. He knew him from his runs to the Streets of Brentwood group. Nick had a wicked sweet tooth and would trade anything for a candy bar.

The kid was hyperventilating, his voice shaky. "You promised, Emily. We said we wouldn't let either of us turn. Do it."

She raised the rifle and centered it on Nick's forehead. Her finger rested on the trigger. Her hand shook as she applied pressure and closed her eyes. As she pulled the trigger, Seth stepped over and yanked the gun up. Her finger jerked and the bullet ricocheted across the pavement.

She pulled the gun away. "What in the hell are you doing? We promised we would take care of the other." The woman wiped tears out of her eyes and glared at him.

Seth stepped up to her and grabbed the weapon. "He isn't dead yet. Or undead." He looked down at Nick. "The wound doesn't look that bad, I've seen others survive a lot worse."

When she looked up at him, hope gleamed in her eyes. He prayed he was right. He'd only seen it work once. He gently put a hand on her shoulder. "Yes, if he doesn't bleed out he might be okay if we get him to the shopping center. I'm Seth by the way. Seth Ripley."

She took his hand off her shoulder and shook it. "Emily Gray and this is Nick Cruz."

"Nick I know," he replied. A moan carried from the street entrance. The zombs from the strip mall across the street were here. Seth glanced over. They weren't going to make it to his truck and he wasn't sure that Canida would even let them back in with Nick's bite anyway.

"Up on the truck," he yelled to Emily and Nick.

His arm no longer bleeding, Nick hopped up on the truck and scampered to the trailer. Emily followed as if she'd been climbing all her life. Seth joined them a little slower, his boots slipping on the roof of the truck.

"Anyone left up there?" Seth bobbed his head toward the roof of the Safeway. The moans and stench below were becoming overwhelming. He heard nothing above.

"Everyone was down here," Emily answered. "They must have come down to help the driver. Maybe he was infected when he got here."

"Up it is then."

A rope ladder was shaky in the best of times, and this wasn't the best of times with the horde below yanking the rope back and forth. Nick climbed like a monkey and helped Emily up next. Then they disappeared. Seth felt his boots slipping on the rope. Suddenly, a body fell past him, bounced off the edge of the truck, and hit the pavement with a thud and a crack of its skull.

"Nope, the driver was up here," two voices chimed.

"Lord, please tell me he was one of the undead."

◆◆◆

I helped Ripley up the last of the rope ladder and we pulled it to us, playing tug of war with the zombies for a few moments until they lost interest since nothing human was coming their way, and shambled across the asphalt. I turned and eyed the rooftop. The truck driver had knocked things over but it still looked pretty intact from what I remembered from my last visit.

I watched as Nick found a first-aid kit. He came running over. Taking the box, I found the hydrogen peroxide, gauze, and tape.

"This is going to hurt," I told him, pouring it quickly over the wound. His yelp and cursing brought a smile to my lips. "Hey, I don't lie."

"You'd make a terrible mom, you know," he complained.

Just like that, the smile died. "So I've been told." I tightened the gauze and taped it in place. The wound didn't look too bad, just a couple of teeth indentations, a few barely breaking the skin. Maybe the man was right. Maybe Nick would be fine. But just in case, I was keeping watch.

Pulling the walkie-talkie off my belt, I checked in with the command post. Nick pleaded with his eyes, but I knew we had to tell them he'd been bitten. We couldn't afford more people coming to our rescue. By dawn, we would know, and that's what I told the base.

"I'll report in at sunrise." Finishing the call, I clicked off the walkie.

Nick wandered away toward the food stores. I let him. When the dark thoughts hit me, I'm not good company. Something Seth obviously didn't know, since he sat down next to me and handed me a container of baby wipes. Damned if I were going to cry in front of a stranger. Being infertile didn't have as much of a gut punch in a world where having a baby was beyond stupid.

"Thanks," I mumbled, grabbing the box.

"No, problem," he said. "I figured you might like to lose the zombie guts."

I ran my fingers through my hair and came away with bits and pieces of flesh. "Oh, yuck."

Glancing over at Seth, I groaned inside. Mr. Clean and Sparkly even had bright-white teeth when he smiled at me. I took a deep breath. Looks weren't everything, but they sure could take your breath away from time to time. Dark hair just brushed his shoulders. And my, what broad shoulders they were. Hazel eyes shone out of a tanned face.

"There's a shower in the corner. Probably cold water, but it's still warm outside. Unless you want to wait until dark," he replied, shrugging his shoulders.

I wiggled, while my back itched from what I was sure was blood running down it. "Nope, now is fine. You'll watch Nick?" No way was I taking a shower in the dark with just me, Seth, and the, maybe infected Nick around.

Seth nodded and I decided to take time to get cleaned up. Across the rooftop, Nick rummaged through the food stores. Even if they had been low, there were only three of us. We should have plenty to last until... well, until.

Swallowing past the lump in my throat, I grabbed a towel and some clean clothes from a basket. The shower was a wooden box with a door.

Stepping inside, I spotted the jerry-rigged showerhead hooked to a hose running down the side of the building.

Tossing the clean clothes over the top of the wood wall, I threw my dirty clothes over to the rooftop. A twist of a knob and cool water rained down on my head. With the heat of the day and the gunk in my hair, the water was great. Running fingers through my hair, the blood, guts, and horror of the day washed away.

I'd certainly come a long way from a Victorian mansion in San Francisco to a wooden box of a shower in the middle of a zombie nowhere land. If I closed my eyes, I could still see the marble shower walls imported from Italy, the custom rain showerheads, and music piped in from an over-the-top luxury sound system. Laughing, I grabbed a bar of soap off a makeshift shelf. I wouldn't trade right now for all the marble in the world that came with the baggage I was well rid of.

Turning the knob, the water petered out to drips. The sun beat down on my head. Birds twittered from a nearby tree. I lathered up, turned the water back on, and rinsed.

I turned off the water one last time and looked up at the sunlight behind my closed lids. The sunshine dried me off better than the plushest Egyptian cotton towel at a couple hundred dollars apiece from a pricey, high-end department store. Constantly telling Michelle to seize the moment, maybe I should take my own advice more often. The sunshine, the birdsong, and fresh breezes were free for everyone.

My short hair was dry with a few swipes of the ragged towel over my head. My body was as well with a few more swipes. There hadn't been any undergarments so I'd have to make do and wash mine. Pulling on a tank top my nipples showed clearly through the thin material. I pulled on a T-shirt as well. Better. Then I yanked on some jeans that almost fit. I'd need a belt or a piece of rope. That felt good too. I'd dropped four pants sizes in the past six months. I hadn't been a size six since high school.

Getting out of the shower, I sat down on a chair and pulled on socks and my own boots. At a man's laugh, I looked up. Seth was over by the food with Nick. It looked like they were putting together lunch. Good, I was starved. I had to laugh at that too. Who knew you could kill zombies, and then turn around and eat? And enjoy it. Flavors were richer. Good smells were deeper. The thought of every meal being your last could do that to you.

CHAPTER FOUR

Man's soul is bared in bright sunlight.
His deeds visible to all, enemy or friend.
Choices are made to be lived by,
deep in his heart and until death.
— Seth Ripley

The setting of the sun brought relief from its bright rays, but not the warmth of the day. It continued into the night. After all this time, Seth was still amazed at the constant nighttime warmth in the summer months in the far East Bay.

Sure, Oakland got hot sometimes, but that bay breeze whipped up and evenings could be downright chilly in the middle of August. He'd been to an Oakland A's game and needed a hooded sweatshirt and a jacket in mid-summer. He sighed. Just one more thing to miss in the after Z time. He'd really liked baseball.

The day had passed pretty well, considering he was a stranger to Emily and just an acquaintance to Nick. He and Emily had taken turns walking the edge of the roof, checking for trouble. He could tell the undead were still congregating below. Every time the woman looked over the edge, the moans would rise in tempo and volume. The scrape of nails and flesh-bare bones on the facade of the building sent shivers up his spine. The stench of dead flesh came and went with the random breezes.

He turned his head at the sound of quiet arguing from Emily. *What was her pre-Z story?* She was strength and fragility wrapped up in one hot woman. At the moment, she was arguing with Nick about sleeping. The boy wanted his turn at standing guard. He swallowed the burr in his throat. The kid had to know they were standing guard against what he might become just as much as the monsters below.

"I want to help."

"I need you to sleep. You hardly ate any dinner and what you did eat came back up. Don't make this harder on me than it has to be, please."

"But, Emily," the boy's pleas carried over the rooftop.

"Nick, I'm hoping it is just the heat and not the virus. But we don't know yet, do we? I know we're partners, but I'm your elder too. Go to sleep now."

The boy conceded and flopped down on a cot beneath a canvas canopy. Emily squatted by a small grill and started a fire. He was confused for a moment until he realized she was making it so they could see Nick from a distance, not face him in the dark up close. Praying, his lips moved silently as he sent up a fervid wish to the heavens to spare Nick. To spare them the choice that would have to be made. His hand moved automatically to cross himself.

"What a good Catholic boy you must be."

Emily's low, friendly tones sent a shiver down his spine and heat everywhere else. He turned away slightly to hide what must be a blush considering the warmth in his cheeks, which had nothing to do with the sweltering air. "Yep, was an altar boy and went to confession every Wednesday. At least I did, until the Z hit. What about you?"

"Episcopalian. Baptist before that."

He turned and stared at her. "You just changed religions like that?"

"I was Baptist when I was a girl. I changed

for Carl. For my husband." Her glance slid from his and stared at the ground.

He looked and saw no ring on her finger. "I'm sorry. The virus?"

"Yes." She stuttered to a stop as if she had more to say but no more words came.

"Did you see him?"

"No, just a photo and the report about him and the hooker in the motel room."

"I'm really sorry," he mumbled and laid a hand on her shoulder.

Her head whipped up and tears glistened in her eyes. "Don't worry. It wasn't the first time. But it was definitely the last." A shaky laugh escaped her, one that proclaimed it was a hurt deeper than she wanted to let on. And now, she had to deal with Nick. The lady had some deep wounds.

He moved away and pulled two campstools over. She plopped down onto hers. He wanted to keep her talking, but nothing seemed like a safe topic.

She spoke up first, "Where are you from? You know—before."

"I lived in Oakland with my mother. She's in a hospital in Concord. All barricaded and safe. Well, as safe as anyone is these days." He swiped a hand across the back of his neck. "And you?"

"I lived in San Francisco with my husband. His parents were nearby. They died of the flu. They were lucky. My parents were attacked trying to reach me across the city. And I already told you about Carl."

Oh, shaky ground again. "What did you do in the city? What were you before?"

Emily laughed. A real laugh. The sound carried and surrounded his body. Her dark eyes shined in the last of the sunset. "I shopped. I went to fundraisers. I was arm-candy for Carl's ego. I was a trophy wife. Part of the idle rich who think if they raise money for needy people they are actually doing something worthwhile, even if they spend more money on the party then they are raising."

His jaw dropped. This Amazon fighting goddess had been a rich man's wife. He didn't see it. She'd been happy to wash in a wood box, throw on whatever she found in the clothes box, and eaten franks and beans like it was a gourmet meal. And she'd handled the gun earlier as if she'd been doing it all her life. She was every young boy's idea of a video-game warrior woman—hot body and all.

She playfully smacked his hand. "You should see your face. What about you? What were you before you became the apocalyptic post office and delivery service?"

"I was the pre-apocalyptic delivery service. That's my truck down there. That's all I've ever been."

He stared out toward the parking lot until her face butted into his view. "Don't do that."

"What?" he asked, truly puzzled.

"That was the before zombies time. None of that matters anymore. We all got a clean slate. We can be whoever we want to be."

"You really believe that? That we can be someone totally different?"

She touched his hand. "Yes I do."

He looked into her eyes. "What if that's what they are? Something new."

Emily pulled away from him as if he were the undead. "They aren't anything. They are dead. This isn't some part of God's grand plan. This is scientists, the president, and people who should have known better, thinking they *were* God."

She stood up. "I'm going to check on Nick."

He stood up as well. "I think I'll do a round of the roof and hop in the shower."

His gaze followed Emily as she reached Nick and sat down beside his cot. Her hand swiped hair out of the boy's face. Even at this distance, he saw her hand shake. The fever must have started.

Seth grabbed his gun and walked to the edge of the roof. Bodies of the undead and truly dead littered the parking lot. He'd noticed before that the zombies went dormant without fresh meat around, unfortunately, either their olfactory or auditory senses were in super drive, because they had no problems detecting humans nearby, and woke up too damned fast.

One circuit around the roof's perimeter showed all was satisfactory. Everyone was asleep and no one was climbing the wall to the temporary sanctuary.

He snatched up a towel and a clean T-shirt to trade for his dirty, sweaty one and hit the shower.

Cleaning off quickly, he dressed and walked over to Nick's cot to check out the boy himself. Nick tossed and turned on the cot, mumbling wordlessly except for the name of Beth.

Emily looked up at him. "His girlfriend back at the base."

"Oh," he whispered, remembering the young girl.

Hours passed with him and Emily switching places between sitting at Nick's bedside and walking the perimeter. He caught a few catnaps in between. As far as he could tell, Emily stayed vigilant through the night.

Finally, about six a.m. by his watch, Emily sat back in a folding chair and nodded off. He stayed by Nick. The fever raged in his body. The cot was drenched with the boy's sweat. The sickly smell wafted on the breeze. His skin lost its ruddy tone and faded to gray. Breaths came farther and farther apart until they stopped altogether.

Seth said a quick prayer begging God to take care of Nick's soul. He stood up and placed his rifle against his shoulder, aiming it at the boy's head. His vision blurred with sweat running into his eyes. *I can't do this. This isn't a zombie. He's a boy. I know his name.*

His finger tightened on the trigger. He applied pressure. He fired.

◆ ◆ ◆

The absence of sound woke me up. I'd been hearing Nick's labored breaths in my subconscious for hours. I knew he was going to die, but sleep let me take the coward's way out. If I slept, he would be fine in my dreams; he would still be there when I woke up.

Moving like an old lady, I pushed out of the chair. In tiny steps, I walked toward the cot. Halfway there and the blast of the gunshot pierced the quiet dawn, shattering it like glass. Nick's body was hidden by the broad shoulders of the man wielding the gun. A sob broke out. I tried to stop it but the tears poured down my face as I rushed to Seth.

I pounded my fists against his back. Incoherent words flew from my lips. The gun fell with a metallic clang and I found myself wrapped in warm, solid male. The last place I wanted to be. In the arms of Nick's executioner. This man who'd taken my responsibility as his own.

My knees gave way and Seth's arms held me as we collapsed to the rooftop. "You didn't let me say good-bye," I screamed to the sky.

His breath tickled as he whispered into my ear. "I didn't want you to have to see him turn. It's better this way. His soul is at peace."

I pushed him away and fell on my butt. "He didn't turn? You killed him?"

"He was dead, stopped breathing. I didn't kill him. Those creatures did."

"Maybe he was in a coma or something." I scooted away, my mind frantically searching for an answer, any answer, but the truth. "You're not a doctor. You don't know."

He moved to a squat, but didn't come toward me. "He didn't have a pulse. He wasn't breathing. He was dead, Emily."

My arms wrapped around my legs and I put my head on my knees. "I know," I whispered. My heart ached with the rest of my body. "I don't want to do this anymore."

"What?" his voice carried to me in the hush of the early-morning world.

"Live."

"Don't say that. Where there is life, there is hope. Someday this will be a chapter in a history book and the survivors will be remembered along with the dead."

A half-sob, half-laugh bubbled up my throat. "Do you really believe that? That we will win? Because, I don't. Not anymore. There are too many of them and too few of us."

My voice broke. "And now, one fewer."

He'd scooted closer and grabbed my hand. "Of course I do. If I didn't, I wouldn't bother getting up in the morning. I wouldn't bother delivering supplies to camps and bases. If I didn't believe, I would think I was just delaying the inevitable. Humans are given the will to survive, no matter what. I have to believe there is a reason for that."

An undead moan echoed from the pavement below, filling my ears. Their stench fouled the crisp morning air like road kill on the highway.

"Yep," I muttered. "The will to survive; no matter what."

Jill James

CHAPTER FIVE

I forced myself to get up off the ground. Things had to be done. I needed to call the base and report in. And I needed to dispose of Nick's body. A sob tried to escape but I pushed it down, refusing to cry right now. It burned in my throat. The time for crying would be later, with everyone else back at the shopping center.

Beth! Just last week Nick had told me about wanting to marry Beth. The young couple had been just waiting for her father to relent because of their age, as if that mattered anymore.

"Why don't you call Jack and I'll take care of Nick?"

A weight left my shoulders. I tried to push it back on where it belonged. "Are you sure? You already had to—to, you know?"

His hands grasped my arms. Their warmth comforted. Just what I needed in this moment. He stared down into my eyes. "Yes, I'm sure. He was your friend."

I pulled away and moved to the far corner of the roof. What to say tumbled over in my head, somersaults of platitudes and useless, meaningless words. Beth was the contact at the base. All transmissions were heard by her, unless she was on a break or asleep. She'd probably slept less than I did last night, waiting for the call this morning. I sighed and crossed my fingers.

Clicking the button on the walkie, I called the base. "This is Emily Gray, reporting in."

A mature male voice replied. "This is Streets of Brentwood. Report?"

"Is Beth there?"

"She finally fell asleep an hour ago. Do you want me to get her?"

"No, please don't."

"Okay," his low, slow gravelly tone said it all. Message received.

"Nick Cruz passed away this morning at..." I glanced at my watch. "0725. Seth Ripley and I need assistance at the Safeway Center."

"Canida has a team ready to go once we heard from you. ETA is thirty minutes. We have a swarm this morning to deal with first."

"Thanks. Over and out." I clicked off the walkie. Leaning over the edge of the roofline, I glared down at the horde below, up and shambling along, a moan ratcheting up as they spotted me. Their rancid odor rising as the morning heat rose. Where were they all coming from? We'd cleaned out this area of town months ago.

The splash of liquid and the scent of gasoline reached me. I turned slightly and spotted Seth on the far corner. He'd cleared the area of all except for a blanket wrapped bundle. He put down the gas can and took a lighter out of his pocket.

"Wait," I yelled across the roof. He looked up and stopped.

Running over, I pulled back the edge of the soaked blanket and dug into Nick's pocket. I pulled out a small jewelry box. I covered him back up and moved away.

"It's for his girlfriend." As if a small black velvet box needed an explanation.

"Do you want to stay?"

I nodded and moved to Seth's side. He flicked the lighter and touched it to the blanket. With a whoosh, it caught fire and flames danced across the fabric. The soft blue color faded as my eyes filled with tears.

I turned my view to the sky when the wrapped bundle turned black. The smoke rose and blew away in a small breeze.

"Good-bye Nick."

An hour later, two trucks pulled into the parking lot, and men and women jumped out. In short order, all was cleared. The dead and undead alike were piled up and incinerated. The only way we could ever be sure. Burying left the worry of contaminating the water table, not to mention the fear of missing even one of the reanimated. As it was, we were probably polluting the air we breathed. Not many choices left.

Part of the team had climbed to the roof and organized the supplies to take with us; they wouldn't be needed here for the foreseeable future. Maybe never. The location wasn't secure and twenty-five people paid for that mistake. Twenty-six including Nick. The commander's voice over the walkie-talkies ordered the buildings demolished. A man named Paul Luther grabbed a crate out of the truck. He'd been a demolition expert in the army with the commander. The army left us with enough C-4 to blow up the whole town, or so I'd heard.

"Fire in the hole."

I ducked down behind a truck. The noise of the blast ricocheted across the silent town like a sonic boom in the desert. Dust clouded the parking lot, and moans started up across the road. Jumping up, I glanced quickly at the collapsed front of the old supermarket. No one would be able to use the death trap again. By winter, with the rain, the store would just fall in upon itself.

Moans grew louder as a horde shuffled and stumbled into the parking lot. We got off a few shots until Paul ordered us into the trucks to fall back. A couple of men stood behind the vehicles with flamethrowers. They covered a few in flames and their sloppy running around did the job of igniting the rest. Flamethrowers were designed to take out live people, as sick a thought as that may be. Zombies are dead beings. You can't cremate with a flamethrower, just kind of melt them all together, and then go in and do mercy shots. Yes, it was as gross as it sounded. Thank God, I hadn't had time for breakfast.

Moving in to finish them off, I bumped into Seth. The firelight coated his olive skin. His eyes narrowed as he shot each undead in the head. I did my share, saying *I'm sorry* in my thoughts, something I hadn't done in months.

We stepped back as the moans died to nothing. Seth grabbed into his shirt and pulled out a crucifix. He kissed it and closed his eyes in prayer. I whipped my head around, making sure nothing got the man while his eyes were closed. I wanted to roll my eyes at his stupidity but something stopped me. Something I hadn't felt in . . . in forever, remorse. *When did I lose my empathy? When had I forgotten these things had been people? That they hadn't asked for any of this, anymore than I had.*

Paul held his hand up for silence. Nothing filled the air except for the wind and the crackle of fire consuming flesh. I heaved a sigh. I was too worn-out to do more killing of zombies today. Everyone talked in whispered tones as they climbed into the trucks.

"You can ride with me," Seth said, standing at my elbow.

"Thanks, I would like that." Really, I would. I needed silence right now. I needed to rehearse in my head what I would say to Nick's girlfriend, Beth. I reached for the box in my pocket. It weighed a thousand pounds sitting there.

We climbed inside and Seth started the truck. He put it into reverse and backed up. Silence filled my ears.

"Shouldn't you have that annoying beep, beep, beep sound for backing up?"

He grinned. "Yeah, real annoying when it attracted the undead, too. I disabled it."

With a big sweep of the steering wheel, we turned around and got behind the trucks from the base. We moved slowly out of the shopping center and stopped in the middle of the road. The riders in the back of the trucks jumped down and used knives, machetes, and crossbows to take out a few stragglers. Looking at the shopping center across the road I was sure we'd be back to demolish that one too. The center was too open to protect. Not for the first time I noted this had been a quaint town before the Z. The kind with 2.2 kids and a picket fence.

Seth seemed to read my mood. No more words were said on the trip back to The Streets of Brentwood. I practiced a dozen ways to tell Beth her boyfriend was gone and all the words just died in my mind as too callous to speak. My fingers rubbed the box in my pocket. My heart stuttered to a stop. I looked up, and we were almost there, leaving the Bypass and turning onto the road the Streets sat on.

"Should I give her the ring or not? Maybe it will hurt more to know he was going to give it to her. Maybe it will help to know he had it for her. I suck at this heart stuff. I have nothing to measure it against."

Seth turned to look at me, his hazel eyes bright and shiny. "Give it to her. It's all she has left."

"Thanks," I said, swallowing hard.

The process to get inside took forever and no time at all. We drove the circle until Seth pulled up in front of the old movie theater. A young girl rushed out of the building, her legs pumping and arms swinging. Her head whipped back and forth between the trucks until her gaze locked on mine.

I took a deep breath and hopped down from the vehicle. "Beth, I'm—,"

Slap.

I hadn't even see it coming until my head snapped back. Seth stepped forward but I put up my hand to stop him.

"You bitch! You got him killed. He trusted you to have his back. I told him Miss Big Bucks wouldn't protect him."

She started to fall, but her father rushed forward and grabbed her limp body. He squatted, his daughter cradled in his arms. Beth's eyes fluttered open and filled with tears. My vision blurred as my own tears fell down my face. Nick had been my friend, a good friend, but to Beth he'd been so much more.

"What happened?" Beth's words whispered in the air between us.

"He got bitten. The bite was so little, we thought he had a chance. But the fever came and he died. We—we didn't let him turn."

She sat up. "Did you—?"

"No," I said, turning to Seth. "He did it."

Seth nodded. I reached into my pocket and pulled out the little velvet box and handed it to Beth. "I haven't seen it but Nick talked about it a lot when we were out on patrol. This was meant to be yours."

My nose burned holding back more tears. Beth's own poured freely down her face as her trembling fingers opened the box and took out a beautiful sapphire ring.

"Put it on, sweetheart," her father said. "It's yours."

The young girl slid it on her ring finger and stared at it. "Oh, Nick." Her voice cracked as she huddled into a ball and screamed her boyfriend's name over and over. Her words becoming muddled and meaningless and hoarse as her voice died.

I couldn't take anymore. Jumping to my feet, I strode away toward the gardens. Faster and faster. Until I was running. I couldn't run far enough or fast enough to escape Nick's death. Falling onto a bench, I hung my head to let all the tears I'd been holding back fall. Great sobs came, leaving me with dry heaves and every bone in my body hurting. Why? Why now? I'd seen more death in the past six months than I'd seen in my whole life. I hadn't cried when Carl died. I hadn't cried when my parents were killed, I'd been too scared and on the run for my life. I'd cried a little in the first days here as someone was taken down by the skinbags or died of something that just weeks before would have been taken care of with a trip to the doctor. But this. This hurt to my soul. Nick had been a child. A child forced to be a man before his time. And now his time was over.

"Are you okay?" Seth's calm voice spoke behind me.

I scrubbed my face with my hands. "Do you have a big family?"

He raised an eyebrow, as if lost by my random tangent. "I have lots of cousins and aunts and uncles. At least, I did. Don't know right now. But yes, a big family."

"I had a mom and a dad. Then I got married and had Carl and his parents. I had a few friends, for events and stuff, none just to be a friend. No one close. Nick was like a little brother. It's like I've lost a part of me. I feel as if I should have done something more for him. Moved faster. Been closer. Something."

He took my hand. "We all feel like that. It's a game of what if that you can't win. What if the Z virus never came? What if the dead didn't rise again? What if I shot faster, sooner, more? We all just do the best we can and leave the rest to God."

"God?" I jerked my hand away. "You've got to be kidding me. If this is God's answer, then I really want to know what the fuck the question was."

Jill James

CHAPTER SIX

All is wrong with a world where the dead don't rest.
All is right with a world with a graceful woman beheld.
It is wrong to blame God for men's mistakes.
It is right to ask God to right men's errors.
— Seth Ripley

By the time dusk fell, fires sprang up in trashcans evenly spaced the length of the mall. Small puddles of glowing red and yellow highlighted the overwhelming darkness of no light pollution. More than two hundred people gathered to remember Nick Cruz. Commander Canida stood in front of the theater with Beth and her father, Jim Evans. They were the closest thing to family that Nick had. He'd lost everyone to the virus and the flu before.

Silence filled the area except for a few crying babies. The crowd stood with bowed heads as Canida told all of Nick's sacrifice. Beth's sobs rolled over the group.

I bowed my head but I refused to pray to a God I no longer believed in. The God of my childhood didn't bring us zombies and he didn't seem to be rescuing us from them either. The commander's words were just mumbles in my head as my own memories of Nick played across my mind. The tales of playing football in this small town, of his family and friends before the world went to hell. His telling of the legends of a local bandit and hidden caves. I smiled at the remembrance of my friend's stories of playing Joaquin Murietta and of a little brother being the law officer to catch the bad guy, trapped in his cave hideout. His stories brought this middle of nowhere town to life for me.

A warm hand settled on my shoulder. I jumped and opened my eyes. Seth stood beside me, his arm across my shoulders. Snuggling in closer, I caught Canida's last words, as he raised a cup.

"Live life to the fullest. We all only have today. Raise your glass for all those lost at the Safeway Center. Raise it for Nick."

"For Nick," murmured from hundreds of throats. "For today."

The crowd broke up and several women went to Beth with soft, whispered words. The young girl stood taller and her tears dried up. The girl became a woman before my eyes. A woman who'd lost her man. Childhood washed away in an instant. The pain of it ripped across me. I moved away from Seth and stood in line to try to say something that didn't sound trite and overused. I'm sorry seemed meaningless as it always has. Just words, but I used them anyway.

"Beth, I'm so sorry. Nick was my friend. If you need anything. Anything at all."

Her smile broke my heart. As if the earlier yelling had purged her anger. "Emily, Nick talked about you all the time. You were his friend too. I'm so sorry. I know you had Nick's back just like he had yours."

She rubbed her stomach. "I've told my father, so it's okay to tell you. I'm having Nick's baby."

My mouth dropped open. Her smile fell at seeing what I'm sure was utter disbelief and condemnation on my face. "That's wonderful news, Beth. I'm so happy for you." The lies died on my tongue. The words refused to continue.

"Thank you, Emily," Beth's voice lost its happy tone.

I moved on, at a loss for words. Beth was sixteen and alone. Well, not totally, she had her father and the community here. A baby who would be a remembrance of Nick. A helpless baby, in the middle of hell on Earth.

Music started up in the center of the green, grassy swath in the middle of the mall. A guitar and banjo softly played Nick's favorite song; the one about a boy and a girl and young love. Beth took her father's hand and they slowly swayed to the soft melody. He bowed his head over her and she pulled herself tight into his chest.

Seth held out a hand. I grabbed it and pulled him to the impromptu dance floor of plywood sheets. The music struck a chord deep inside. I'd never had a young love. The commander's words echoed in my head. We only had today, tomorrow might never come. We had no guarantees, not anymore; if we'd imagined we had them before, it had all been a lie. It'd taken the zombie apocalypse to make me see that the future was an ethereal dream of impossibility.

Dance after dance flew by. Seth's arms held me gently as a slow song started. I looked up into eyes shining in the moonlight and with something else—passion. His fingers caressed my back as we moved around the other couples, tingle running up and down my spine. The area was packed with people, the only ones missing were the guards on the rooftops, and someone would spell them later so they could enjoy some food and company.

Overwhelmed with the mass of people, I pulled away and fell into a chair. My ears were humming with the buzz of the crowd. I was divided. One part of me loved the festivity, the celebration of Nick's life. But the other part wanted to find a corner to hide in and cry. To mourn the loss of a young boy forced to be a man too soon, to die too soon.

The music's tempo changed to a fast-paced country song. I looked up and spotted Seth line-dancing with Michelle. Even with the lack of a future to worry about, I don't make split-second decisions. So why did I know right then where I wanted the evening to end. With my body wrapped around Seth's in hot, passionate, sweaty, sex. My heart raced a million miles a second. If I could organize a gala event for hundreds at a moment's notice, surely I could find some privacy for Seth and me for one evening.

My body sparked with electricity at the thought of Seth, privacy, and more. His eyes had said he would accept my invitation. Jumping up, I marched over to Mrs. Roberts.

"Bobbie, I need a tent for tonight. Please tell me they aren't all parceled out." I crossed my fingers behind my back.

"Sweetie," she said as she touched my arm. "For you, I'll find one." Her glance shot to Seth. "If anyone deserves tall, dark, and handsome over there, it's you."

My face heated up and I thanked the darkness for hiding it. Mrs. Roberts had known me in our former lives. She'd been a shoulder to cry on many of times.

She pulled a notebook out of her pocket. "Looks like I've got a few left. I'll have a couple of boys set one up in your spot."

"Thank you so much." I wrapped my arms around her and squeezed tight. I didn't have my mother anymore, but Mrs. Roberts was an excellent grandmother-surrogate.

Thirty minutes later, the older woman pushed through the crowd to my side. She reached out and squeezed my arm. "All taken care of. You have a good evening." She glanced over across the picnic table to Seth. "Hmmm, a very good evening."

Like a whirlwind, she and Michelle faded into the shrinking crowd. A few dancers still slow-danced in the middle of the Green, but couples and families headed toward bed. My breath caught. Where I wanted to be with Seth. *How do you ask a man to come to your room, even if it is just a tent? Carl had been the cheater, going from affair to affair. I'd never even looked at another man, even once I knew about the infidelity.*

I took a deep breath. "Seth, I know we've just met. But, I don't want you to leave yet." I stuttered to a stop. I sounded as if I was sixteen, instead of almost thirty.

He blushed. Did adult men do that? He looked deep into my eyes and I fell... hard.

"Emily, I would love to stay." His deep voice sent a thrill down my spine and heat to places that hadn't had any heat in a while. A long while.

Seth stood up, grasped my hand, and pulled me tight against his warm body. His lips brushed over mine and a fire roared in my blood. I closed my eyes and breathed in his male scent mixed with rich homemade beer. His skin was warm and musky from dancing.

A whisker-stubble cheek slid along my face, as he whispered into my ear. "Lead the way."

He pulled back slightly and I pointed out the southwest corner of the compound and the breakaway stairs in the center of the building section. "Up there, with the clotheslines."

His arm went around my shoulders as we walked toward the stairs. "Last time I was here, it was all rope ladders and crate pulleys," he whispered.

"We have a lot of kids now. Lots of little ones. Canida ordered steps built. They just push away from the building and fall over if we got overrun."

The steps swayed slightly as we walked to the rooftop. I pulled Seth over to the corner where a tent occupied the usual place of my cot and a tarp I'd fashioned into a lean-to with the help of the pole for the clothesline. Bending down, I moved inside and gasped. My cot was pushed against a canvas wall, with my stuff piled on top. In the middle of the tent was a mattress.

If my face heated any hotter, I would implode. The boys who set up the tent had to have known why I wanted a mattress. Seth bumped into me as he came through the doorway. As I fell I grabbed a hold of him and we both landed on the soft surface. I moaned. I'd forgotten how soft a real bed could be.

"Let me zip up the door," he whispered with a quick kiss on my lips, tasting hot and sweet. Too quick. I wanted more. I fed on his lips. His kisses grew blistering. Heat pooled between my thighs. I wanted him now.

Seth moved away and the sound of the zipper on the tent filled the space. The silence filled me with doubts. *What was I doing? My friend died today. This was wrong.*

Looking up, I saw the same doubts in Seth's eyes. I bit my lip and started to talk. "I'm—"

He sat beside me on the mattress, his arm going around my shoulders. "We don't have to do this. I'm not an animal in need of sex."

I giggled. I couldn't help it. His warm body and eyes full of life and kindness was the furthest thing from the renegades we'd heard about. The rumors of men roaming the wasteland, taking what and who they wanted swirled through the camp weekly.

"I read somewhere that the most sex happens after a funeral. Most people think it is after a wedding, but weddings just usually scare guys off. Worried about the ball and chain thing. But funerals remind everyone that they are still alive."

His hands cupped my face. "I can believe that. We honor those we've lost by continuing on, by living life to the fullest."

His lips touched mine. His breath caressed my face. "Nick is only gone for a while. He has friends to remember him and Beth's baby to carry on his life."

A pang ripped though me at the thought of Nick and Beth's baby. I tossed the regret aside in a second. At least I didn't have to worry about birth control on top of everything else in our torn-apart world.

I wrapped my arms around Seth. "Let's celebrate life."

He fell back to the bed, taking me with him. The few clothes between us were too much. My hands grasped for his shirt and mine. I tossed them aside and ran my fingers over his warm chest. He pulled me close and I reveled in the feel of skin-to-skin contact.

Seth removed my bra and caressed my breasts. Tremors shot through my body. I flung my head back, letting his hands run wild. His fingers skimmed over my nipples. Something between a gasp and a sigh escaped my lips until his mouth found the sensitive peaks. Then, I bit my tongue to hold back the scream of pleasure.

Our fingers fumbled together on our belt buckles. We continued kissing as we each ripped off our pants, only stopping to remove boots and denim.

I rushed back into his arms. He took off my panties and his own underwear. I glanced down with half-closed lids. Seth Ripley was all male. From his taut muscles, to his erection springing from his curly-haired groin, he was hard and tight. Pale flesh pulsated against inky black.

My fingers grasped the firm flesh and I delighted to his gasp of pleasure. Arms wrapped around each other, we again fell to the bed. He kissed me, whispering my name as he found my hot center. My back arched off the mattress as he entered me, every nerve ending firing off pulses of heat, movement, and slick wetness.

Never like this.

Never such heat.

Never such passion.

Never.

Never.

Never.

We moved together as if we'd been making love for years. His mouth found the sensitive spot where neck meets shoulder. I moaned deep. His mouth moved to mine to capture my groans of passion. Electric pulses traveled my skin wherever he touched. His lips. His tongue. His fingers.

I wrapped my legs around him and urged him on; faster and faster. My whispers repeated the command. I dug my fingertips into his shoulders as the rhythm slowed down and sped up, in a tempo guaranteed to make me scream at the apex. In the last seconds, he slowed down and moved deeper, as if that were possible. Closing my eyes, I saw lights dancing behind my lids. The explosion came and took me over the edge. Seth's moans mixed with mine.

"Damn."

My heart stuttered to a stop. Was he regretting our impetuous act? Was he regretting the best sex I'd had in my life?

He rolled off me and covered his eyes with his arm. "I can't believe I was so thoughtless. I didn't even stop for protection."

I propped myself up with an elbow and looked over at him. "Don't, Seth." I pried his arm away from his eyes. I wanted to see his face. I wanted him to see mine.

"I would have said something if it mattered. And you seem like an upstanding guy. I'm sure you would have said something if we had anything to worry about."

He sat up, pulling me with him. "I didn't think about that for a moment. But there are other considerations. Unless you want a baby in the middle of this mess we're living in."

Tears blurred my vision. "A baby is the last thing I have to worry about, Seth. I'm infertile. That's why my husband died with a hooker. Constantly needing to prove there wasn't a problem on his side of the equation."

He took my hands and kissed the tears running down my face. I smiled at him. "So, no more stressing, okay? Don't ruin the first sex I've had in five years."

His stunned look was enough to set me off for round two. Part amazement and part thrill raced across his face, as I tackled him and straddled his hips.

CHAPTER SEVEN

Somewhere in the Delta
East Bay Area, California

"General Peters. We're ready for the next test."
Martin smirked. He'd never been the general of anything, let alone been in a service that had generals. Unless he counted being a supervisor at an auto repair shop, with ex-cons and illegals to order around, and that didn't count for shit.

But, let the world go to hell in a handbasket and the man holding the basket could take any title he wanted. Let the guy have a safe haven in the Delta and the firepower to hold it and men were willing to follow you and call you any damn thing you demanded. Have the balls to hold it all together and the best food, drink, weapons, and women were yours for the taking.

He pushed away from his desk in the safe

room in his bunker. Walking past rows of shelves with canned goods and bottled water, he glanced at the food and smiled as he noted the stock had been rotated on schedule. To fuck up that simple task got you bumped to latrine digging duty—permanently.

He clapped his second-in-command on the shoulder. "Captain Gomez, I hope this test runs better than the last?" His not subtle hint hung in the air between them.

Antonio swallowed audibly and his Adam's apple bobbed up and down in his skinny throat. The man's thin frame shook from head to toe. Martin wouldn't be surprised to hear Gomez's knees knock together.

"You're sure everything is ready?" He squeezed the man's shoulder, feeling the bones grind beneath his fingers. The power play sent an orgasmic thrill through his body. The apocalypse should have happened years ago.

The captain winced, but held firm. "Of course, General."

Peters stepped back, crossing his arms across his chest. "I believe you were sure last time—" His voice boomed across the enclosed space. "And now I've lost four good men and have four extra undead fuckers to deal with, don't I?"

Martin stalked up to the man until they were nose-to-nose, but Antonio held his ground, his shaking subsiding.

"This time I've tried something different. The creatures will be staked on a leash. We can watch their movements with no one in danger."

"Very good, Captain." He patted the man on the cheek harder than necessary. "Perhaps you should have thought of that last time."

"Sir, I told you—um, I let you know there was a chance of failure until we get the right frequency."

"Yes you did, Antonio. But you'd better find it soon. Because I'm running out of patience—and men."

◆ ◆ ◆

Tanya Gomez placed a hand to her brow, to shield the sun's glare from her eyes. She spotted the general and that sniveling, idiotic Antonio coming out of the bunker.

She sighed. So many zombie widows, as they were called, and she was still stuck with a stupid husband. Her glance slid to Martin Peters. There was a man! He saw what he wanted and he seized it. Just like he'd seen her in town long before the zombies came, and seized her.

Her breath caught and she squeezed her thighs together. What a lover. *Muy caliente.* Rough and strong, just like she wanted it, needed it. He was her best so far. She'd had many since her first at fourteen, but none like Martin. His tastes were even more perverted than her own.

Antonio ran up to her, wrapping his arms around her, suffocating her. He swooped in for a kiss. She turned her head at the last second and his perpetually wet lips slid along her cheek. She shuddered as he whispered in her ear.

"*Mi espousa*. My wife. I love you."

She pushed her husband away. "Go do your job. Don't keep the general waiting. You know how angry he gets."

He kissed her quickly before she could stop him. As he ran to catch up with Peters, she wiped her hand across her mouth and dried it on her jeans. Her time was coming. Soon, she'd get rid of the boy and have a man.

Tanya strolled over to the arena with the rest of the people standing nearby. She noted the crowd was smaller than for the last test. She smiled. *Some people were such wimps. A little bloodshed and they couldn't handle it. So what if a few soldiers were killed?*

The ripping.

The tearing.

The moans of the undead as they fed.

She shuddered and squeezed her thighs together.

That night Martin had been a beast as well.

The bloodshed had been more than just a little when the four men were mauled by the zombies. Several men had jumped up with guns ready to fire, but the general had ordered them to stop. The infected were forced into the cages with the rest of the zombs.

That stupid Antonio thought he had a way to control the creatures. She prayed he failed again. Maybe the general would finally end his loser life.

She found a seat near the top of the wooden grandstands. A new fence enclosed the arena after the last debacle. The fresh-sawed wood smell almost covered the stench of the undead. Their moans filled the air. The beasts were leashed to tall stakes in a semicircle around the far edge of the dirt arena.

General Peters strode to the near end, his hand wrapped around a young girl's arm. Tanya squinted. Miranda Stevens. She sat up straighter, a smile on her lips. Miranda was the latest young thing in Martin's bed. He stood tall, his gaze directly to her, and an evil grin on his face. Yes! The stupid girl meant nothing to him. He was hers.

A man yelled from the edge of the arena. "Stop. You can't do this. She's my baby."

General Peters nodded and a man stepped up to the distraught father and a shot rang out across the field. Blood blossomed on his white shirt. The man fell to the ground. A silent moment passed, the crowd leaning forward. He twitched, rolled over, and got to his knees. Falling a few times, the now-undead man stood and lurched toward the general and the young girl.

"Tie him with the others."

Her breath caught and her heartbeat raced. He would take her rough tonight. Do all the things she liked but didn't know how to ask for. The welts and bruises would let everyone know who she belonged to, even Antonio. Especially Antonio.

The girl screamed as she tried to pull away from Peters. "You promised. I did everything you asked. You promised."

He pushed her to the ground. "I make no promises, little girl." A young man came forward and tied her hands behind her back. She started to run. Peters grabbed her by her long hair and his fist connected to her temple. The girl crumpled to the ground.

"Let's get started," he yelled to Antonio.

She laughed as her husband glanced at the young woman on the ground and rushed to the platform with the stereo equipment. Her fingers dug into her thighs. Maybe he would fuck up again and she could finally be through with him after Martin killed him for her.

Her nipples pebbled under her shirt at the thought of being with the general out in the open for all to see. She'd be the first lady of their enclave. Hell, she could aim for Queen of California.

A hum came from the speakers, and then turned into silence except for the barking of every dog on the compound. The creatures in the arena turned in circles, tangling themselves with the ropes around the poles. Black liquid oozed down their arms and legs as they strained against the ropes.

Antonio's fingers flew across the synthesizer. There appeared to be no change in the silence, except for the hum on the edge of her hearing. Enough to make her believe she could almost capture the sound. The zombies pulled on their leashes, fighting to attack each other. Martin walked up to Antonio and shoved him to his knees, pulling his gun out of the holster.

Her husband put his hands up. She just caught his words. "... just some adjustments."

Martin put the gun away. "Better get it right. My patience is wearing thin."

Antonio jumped up and his fingers trembled on the controls. Her teeth ached as he made another adjustment. The zombies stopped moving. They stood and swayed in place, looking at the sky.

Antonio pointed to the girl. Martin spat orders and several men gathered the girl and put her within reach of the monsters, then ran away. The crowd swayed forward in their seats as the sound continued and the undead ignored the fresh meat in their midst.

"Okay, this is what I wanted to show you." Antonio spoke to the general as he spun a dial on the control board.

Her mouth fell open as the creatures all stretched their tethers as far as they could reach— away from the girl. They ignored her completely. All were attracted to the speakers in the trees, like dogs with a treed raccoon. Some fool thought Antonio had made them harmless. The man touched one and lost his hand in the process, blood squirting across the man's face and the dirt of the arena.

Martin pulled his gun and shot the man dead on the spot. A head shot.

He smiled as he put the gun away. Clapping Antonio on the back, Martin grinned. "Amazing. We need to pick a target for practice."

Antonio spun the dial to make the zombies again look to the sky and ignore all the rest. Martin snapped his fingers and directed the men to get the girl out of the center. They snatched her up and looked to him.

"Take her to the guards. It's been a while since they've had some fun."

Tanya rushed to her husband's side. For the crowd's benefit, she gave him a big kiss. "Antonio, you are so brilliant."

Martin moved to the other side. "So, Antonio, my friend, what do you need for a practice run at a real target?"

CHAPTER EIGHT

Seth managed to keep Emily in the Streets of Brentwood compound the first day, but by the second day after Nick's death, he could see she was going stir crazy. She'd helped her friend, Michelle with laundry detail until there wasn't a pair of dirty underwear left in the compound. He'd suggested she help her friend, Bobbie Roberts organize a group of teenagers who'd wanted some space of their own. With some shuffling around, the teen group soon settled on a rooftop away from the grown-ups, with empty rooftop space on either side. A pirate flag soon hung down from the store façade and cheering wafted across the open mall as the fabric of the skull and crossbones cracked in the wind.

She was now talking to Bobbie and the hard glances she shot his way warned him he wasn't going to like whatever plan she'd hatched to get out of the enclosed space of the shopping mall.

"Bobbie and I think the camp needs more

tents." Emily stood in front of him, hands on hips as if waiting for his argument. At that moment, he'd gotten a clearer picture of her married past. If she were spoiling for a fight, he wasn't going to give it to her. He'd seen her in action. The woman could take care of herself and cover his back too.

"I know there are several sporting goods places in town and nearby, but I'm sure they've been picked clean."

The older woman nodded. "Emily and I were thinking it's time to start clearing some houses and getting some supplies. Lots of families in this community must have camped. We could find camping stoves, lanterns, maybe even those little pop-up tent things."

"From what Nick told me..." Emily's jaw clenched with a teeth-grinding sound as she paused at the kid's name. "A lot of people owned guns in this town. We might as well collect what we can."

Bobbie spoke up again. "The patrols are already out and about, but I know Joe and Bob waited around to see if you wanted them to go with you. Josh and Suz volunteered too. The Logans said they would be ready when you are."

"We should help them," he said.

"I'll go get my stuff," Emily said, giving him a quick hug.

He watched her long strides carry her to the breakaway stairs.

"That woman needs space. She might have married money, but she didn't come from it, if you know what I mean."

Seth gave the older woman his attention at her unexpected words. "I thought it was one of those 'combining dynasties' things."

She laughed, throwing her head back. "Oh no, Emily was doing secretary work at her dad's law office. Carl spotted her, decided it was time to make the next generation of Grays, and married her."

"So he fell in love, just like that? Not that I can't see the attraction, because I certainly can."

Bobbie snorted. "No love match there. Oh, maybe she felt something for him at first. Taken in with the things money can buy. But Carl was only concerned in how Emily looked and dressed and acted. He needed the right someone to play the part of Carl's wife. Unfortunately, she found out the only person Carl loved was Carl."

"How did you get to know Emily?"

"I lived near the Grays. I met Emily at a party and I could see right away that she needed a friend, someone who wasn't after her connections. I watched as Emily started to die inside when Carl started stepping out. I haven't seen her as happy as she's been killing skinbags. She finally found something she can do, all on her own. So don't take that away from her. She's no 'princess in a tower'. Go out there, watch her back, but don't let her know you are watching her back."

"I will," Seth replied softly as Emily ran up to them.

She slid to a full-stop with her backpack strapped on, crossbow in hand. Giving him a grin and a quick kiss, her smile grew when he pulled her in close. "Suz and Josh are ready at the exit. They found a big truck for us to go out in."

Emily gave Bobbie a hug and they strode over to the exit at the cargo containers. Josh sat at the wheel of a super-sized black truck, with his sister, Suz in the passenger seat. Joe and Bob were already in the bed of the truck, so Emily and Seth hopped up on the tailgate and joined them. Bob slapped the roof and the truck headed out.

"Are we going to the apartments?" Emily asked the guys.

Joe shook his head. "Josh doesn't think we'll find a lot of camping stuff there and the parking lots are too tight. No room to maneuver. We could get trapped there."

Emily nodded. "Makes sense. So where?"

"We're heading over past the church. Nice neighborhood there. I've seen a bunch of motor homes and trailers in the area."

Seth glanced around as they passed the church. A giant X in red marred the pristine whiteness of the doors, which were covered with crossed plywood to stop any zombies from using the church as a nest.

He saw Emily's shoulders tense as they passed a small school and playground. He could sympathize; he hated when they found children undead. It was all kinds of wrong to have to put down little ones.

The play yard looked deserted except for a

few mounds of decaying flesh held together by shreds of clothing. He looked away, swinging the rifle Joe had handed him in a semicircle to survey the neighborhood for threats.

"Stop," Emily cried, hopping out of the truck bed before the vehicle came to a complete stop.

Seth jumped down to cover her. "What?"

She jerked her head toward the Confederate flag hanging from a porch flag holder. "A candy bar and a pack of gum say we find a weapon cache there."

He smiled at the mention of the only currency that now mattered and counted for anything, the things now in short supply. "I'll take that bet. I say they bugged out when the shit hit the fan and took the guns with them."

Emily grinned. "I accept. Just know that I love Hershey's."

She reached out and knocked on the door, followed with her ear against the wood. Another knock and she grabbed the doorknob. Turning it, the door swung open. She pushed her crossbow over her shoulder and pulled a gun from her holster. Standing still, she sniffed deeply. Holding up her fingers in the okay sign, they all filed into the house, Joe left standing on the porch when they went inside.

He and Emily moved through the living room to the kitchen. He heard the Logans as they proceeded down the hall to the bedrooms. Like the police in the past, doors opened, followed by the "clear" call echoing in the empty house. A lost reminder of a lost world.

The kitchen reeked of spoiled food smell. The kind that made you catch your breath and wish you hadn't. They'd learned early on to leave refrigerators closed. Scratching sounds in the cabinets broadcasted there wouldn't be any pantry findings in this kitchen. The small animals were taking back their fields and meadows that had been covered by suburbia.

Seth heard closets opening and closing down the hall. He and Emily moved to the door in the kitchen leading to the garage. He spotted a vintage Corvette and an enormous gun safe.

Emily squealed like a girl in a jewelry store. Something must have spooked the tenants, because the safe stood open, guns and ammo spilling out like pirate loot.

"Yes." She hopped up and down. "I knew it. You owe me candy," she sang out.

Seth moved over to the garage door and pushed it up. Light spilled into the open space, highlighting the cherry-red car, the safe, and tools scattered across a work bench designed for more than a basic do-it-yourselfer.

Looking up, he spotted belongings in the rafters. Wincing, he jumped onto the hood of the 'vette with a metallic ping and denting of the hood, apologized in his head, and pulled down tents, cots, a cook stove, and crates.

He jumped to the floor and found a pry bar on the bench. A few tugs and the boxes opened, light falling over mounds of brass casings. Turning, he spotted equipment to make bullets sitting on the workbench.

"Emily, I'm going to get Bob and the others. We need to get this stuff back to the base. We'll be able to make our own bullets."

"Fine, I'll clean out this safe. There're enough weapons here for a gun shop."

◆ ◆ ◆

Half of my body was in the safe when something bumped my foot. "Just a minute, I think this is a box of grenades. I'd like to not blow myself up."

A moan filled my ears and every hair on my body stood up. My bladder wanted to let go and my stomach turned. A hand grabbed me by the ankle and dragged me out of the safe. The stench had bile rising up my throat as the creature held onto my foot, trying to pull it into its mouth.

The reeking skinbag stood up and pulled me with it. The pressure built as the thing gnawed on my boot. Hell no, I wasn't going to go hanging upside down and done in by a bite to my toes.

I brought my other foot around behind the thing's knees, swept it forward, and took that zombie down. Unfortunately, I went down too. Good thing I could jump up faster than a zombie did when you knocked it down.

I jumped up.

Then I jumped down.

Right on his head. With a crunch of bone, my

boot pulverized its head and brains. And I kept on jumping. I was not going to die like Nick. Like Josie. Like Peter. Like Benny. Like the young girl my first week at the camp. Like all the faces and names I could remember since this started. My neighbors in the city. The police officer helping us into the evacuation bus.

"Hell, no," I screamed until I was hoarse. I stopped and looked up. Seth stood in the doorway, with Josh and Suz behind him. They all stood there with their mouths open and guns raised.

"What? Haven't you seen anyone kill a zombie before?" I joked, then my throat seized up and the tears flowed. I turned away, but the tears wouldn't stop. Arms surrounded me and held on tight.

"Are you okay? Are you bit?"

I shook my head, my voice gone. "No. No bites," I whispered.

"It's okay. We all get to freak out a little from time to time. Just makes us human. Today was your turn."

The laughter trickled out between the tears. I stood straighter and pulled away a little. "I'm fine now."

I stared at my gore-covered boot. "Shit, I liked this pair. It took me weeks to break them in."

Seth hugged me with one arm and kissed my cheek. "I'm sorry I left you alone out here. The area looked clear."

I hugged him back. "It's okay. I think I took

care of the problem."

"Yes, you did," Suz voiced from the doorway. "I saw tons of shoes, boots, and clothes in the bedrooms. The family must have been packing to bug out."

Grabbing my knife out of my pocket, I sliced the laces off and toed off my boots. Skirting the mess by the safe, I walked into the house. I turned at the last second. "Before *it* showed up, I found a box of grenades in the safe."

Suz grabbed my hand and pulled me down the hallway. Suz Logan is strong. She looks like a beauty queen with her sun-bleached blonde hair and bright blue eyes, but I've seen her take down five zombies on her own, with a stick and a knife. She and her brother came to Brentwood early in the Z virus infestation. They'd lived in Concord, but it was gone now. The only people left were pockets of survivors too stubborn to leave, surrounded by the undead. The only major thing left there was a hospital. A few doctors and nurses refused to leave their unmovable patients and offered help to the survivors left behind.

Suz and her brother Josh were inseparable. They never went on a mission without the other. She'd told me even before the zombies, they'd been alone, the last members of their family. Most had died of the flu epidemic. She and her brother had been sick too. They'd woken up and everyone else was dead.

We went into a bedroom and I was hit by flying boots. Suz just laid into me.

"That was stupid. You know that, right? While you were stomping the hell out of ghoulie number one, did you even stop to think about numbers two through one hundred that might have been out there? I've already mourned Nick this week; I'm not adding you to the list."

My mouth fell open. *Damn, I'm so stupid. I wasn't thinking.*

"Suz, I'm so sorry. I'm usually better than that."

"Damn straight, you are." She punched my arm. "And don't you forget it. I taught you everything you know."

I winced. "Yes, ma'am."

Pulling the boots on, I glanced around the room and at the stuff on the bed. Wow! Camouflage pants and jackets, Kevlar vests, arm guards, shin guards, and even protective vests made for a woman filled the bed to overflowing. I grabbed one and held it up.

"This is so going to be mine."

Looking around at all this preparedness, I couldn't help wondering what had happened to the occupants. There wasn't any damage, so they hadn't been attacked in the house. But they hadn't left and taken all their stuff either. Had they been ready to go and ran out to help a neighbor? Had they needed some last-minute item and just never made it back? I hated all the not-knowing in this new world. Lives just stopped, like a broken clock, and there was no one left to restart the world.

CHAPTER NINE

Concord Hospital
Concord, California

Dr. Shannon Drake cradled Carla Ripley's thin hand between her own. Not that the woman knew she was there, but it comforted Shannon to spend a few minutes each day with the comatose patient. Frantic from morning to night, these moments with Mrs. Ripley calmed her. She talked to the woman and heard answers in her head.

She sighed. "We should be seeing Seth again soon, Carla. He comes about every other week."

The son had brought her in months ago after she'd escaped from Oakland and fell into a diabetic coma on the trip out. Shannon still couldn't figure out how she was still alive. The doctors finally decided it had to do with the flu epidemic she had survived. For whatever reason, the patient lingered on.

"Maybe you're the lucky one, not us. You get to sleep away this whole nightmare." She laughed. "Maybe when you wake up this will all be over."

Everyone looked to Shannon for answers. After the first wave of attacks, she was the senior doctor left in charge. Senior, ha! Wasn't that a joke? At thirty-five, she was in charge of an entire hospital. They all looked to her for answers, and she just didn't know them. She didn't want to be a leader, just a doctor. But, choices had been taken away, along with every other freaking thing. Food. Medical supplies. Clean water. Everything was in short supply.

She rubbed her eyes. They felt as if they were sand-blasted. Not enough hours in the day to get everything done. On top of the usual insanity of a hospital, she also had to organize food and supplies with Ripley, make sure the generator kept working, and worry about zombies.

She was just so tired. When did it all just stop? When did she get a break? Not since her intern days had she felt so bone-weary.

"Carla, you have a wonderful son there, you know?" She patted the woman's bruised hand with gentle strokes. "We would have never made it without his deliveries."

A nurse came into the room. "Dr. Drake? The patient in 2F is having a heart attack."

Shannon put Carla's hand down gently on the covers and jumped up. There hadn't been a code blue alarm, not since the beginning of the Z virus. That one had every zombie in the area at their front door. After that, a nurse ran and got the doctor. She still wondered how they could hear it all the way outside. The damned things had supersonic hearing or something.

After thirty minutes of trying, Shannon stepped away from the patient. "Damn it. Who was responsible for charging the defibrillator?"

A young man stepped forward. "I was."

She read his nametag. "Well, Todd. If you had been paying attention when you were charging, you would have noted that the charge wasn't holding, the button going back to red as soon as it was unplugged."

"Dr. Drake. I'm sorry."

"Todd, I'm sure you are. But that doesn't bring Mr. Jamison back, does it?"

Todd smirked.

Shannon smiled unwillingly. "Okay, you know what I mean." She pulled her gun out of the holster and handed it grip first to the young man. "Mr. Jamison's non return is now your responsibility."

She left the room and stood by the closed door. She waited for the slight sound of the silenced weapon and the young man's sobs before she headed upstairs to visit the rest of her patients. That he had cried meant there was hope for him yet.

◆◆◆

"Work, dammit," Jed Long yelled at the radio as he pounded on the side of the casing, and then stopped to rub it like he'd hurt the inanimate object. He'd started as a janitor at Concord Hospital until the Z virus turned everything upside down, and Dr. Drake had discovered his hobby was ham radios. After that, he was the communications hub for the Far East Bay Area.

Thanks to Seth Ripley, he'd been able to make a run to his apartment downtown, and return with all his radios and equipment. He swiped long hair back behind his ears. Now, he was connected to the area and the world. Not that there was a lot of world left out there. Spain and Portugal had gone dark early on. Cornwall seemed like the only place left in Great Britain, must be the rough terrain he'd seen pictures of in school. Paris fell in the first few days. The flu vaccine may have been meant for the United States, but once it mutated into a lethal virus, worldwide travel took care of the rest of the planet.

Asia held on the longest; with so many people vaccinated for the bird flu, it took another mutation to do them in. Before they went dark, China was reporting deaths and risings in the hundreds of millions. He shuddered. Thankful the country was on the other side of the world. The thought of hundreds of millions of undead was enough to make him never sleep again.

He pushed his glasses back up his nose and

turned the dial on the radio calibrated for the local camps and compounds. A shrill hum vibrated into his headset. He twitched and yanked them off, slamming them to the desktop. The hum had been infiltrating the radio for days.

He rubbed his jaw. The hum set his fillings to vibrating, threatening to fall out, and unless a dentist miraculously appeared, he wasn't getting new ones anytime soon. The door behind him opened, and Jed spun around in his chair. That young nurse, Amy peeked around the door.

"Hi, Jed. Talking to anyone interesting?" She talked while chewing and popping her bubble gum. He wondered where she kept getting some. And how she managed to walk and chew at the same time, when it seemed like her brainpower would only be capable of one or the other.

"Now I am," he said with a smile.

She smiled back, swallowed her gum, got down on her knees, and swallowed him.

A while later, she sat up on the mattress they'd fallen on to and handed him his glasses. She looked around as a hum filled the space like feedback from a microphone.

She covered her ears, while Jed jumped up and turned down the sound on his radio. The hum grew dimmer, but remained. He pulled on the headset. He switched frequencies and it died. His fingers played with the dial, bringing the sound back. Glancing at the chart thumb-tacked to the wall, he saw it was the location for the small enclave across town. A few stubborn holdouts were trying to survive atop a small strip mall just off the freeway. A couple of old men and their cult-like followers who chose to live by the mantra of at least two women for every man and no woman alone. The only reason they still existed was drivers like Ripley who'd take supplies to them from time to time.

He pressed the mic. "Rob's group. Do you read me? I'm getting feedback. Anyone there?"

"They—everywhere. Can't—them off. God—us."

"Rob's group. This is Jed at Concord hospital. Can you read me?"

Nothing but static. Even the hum was gone.

Jed jumped up, pulling the headset with him. He jerked back, ripped it off, and threw it on the desk. He grabbed his pants and yanked them on, throwing Amy's clothes at her. "Get dressed. We have to find Dr. Drake."

CHAPTER TEN

"Man, I hate new boots," I muttered, swishing my toes in the bucket of sun-warmed water. The boots Suz had thrown at me earlier in the day were brand new. Correction. They had been brand new; they were well broken in now. I had the blisters to prove it. Looking away from the pink-tinged water, I stared at Seth instead. He turned on the lantern and hung it from the tent pole.

Squatting, he took my feet out of the water and gently dried them, patting with a towel. I sighed. The feet must be an erogenous zone I'd never heard about. I leaned back on my elbows and enjoyed the unexpected pleasure. Carl had been all 'me, me, me'. I would have never thought to get such tenderness out of him.

I stifled a yawn. What a long day. But we'd brought back ten truckloads of stuff: food, ammo, guns, and equipment. Closing my eyes, I could still see the acres of tents on the rooftops. A few more trips and everyone would have the comfort of canvas and nylon for defense against the heat we had now and the rainy season to come. Not to mention privacy. My face heated up with a blush.

Sitting up, I ran my fingers through Seth's thick hair. Strands of black, brown, and sun-streaked blond fell through my fingers. I ran my hand behind his neck and pulled him toward me. "Let's go to bed."

He crawled from the foot of the bed like a panther on the hunt. His body heat covered me as he slid along my legs and rested at the apex between them. His hard flesh pulsated against my core.

My fingers ran over his smooth-shaved cheeks. In the middle of everything, he'd found time to shave. Blood heated in my veins and my pulse rapid-fired in a staccato burst. Tears formed and blurred my vision. This was a very kind man.

He sat up and pulled off his shirt. A very hot man, too. Even with the 'mom' tattoo I'd discovered on his chest. I smiled as he pulled off my shirt as well. Unhooking my bra, he lay down and covered me; touching skin to skin. I sighed. I could stay this way forever. Until, he moved and I wanted more.

My fingers tangled in his hair, pulling him close. His lips found mine. His tongue slid along the edge until I opened my mouth and let him in. He tasted of the chocolate bars we'd found at one of the houses. Finding only two meant we got to keep them for ourselves. More than five of something eatable required us to return it to base to be put with the rest of the supplies.

Our tongues slid together and a moan escaped me as his fingers found my nipples. They glazed lightly over them, just like I loved best. His kisses left my mouth and traveled to my earlobe, my shoulder, and the delicate spot in between that had my back arching and warmth flooding my center. Tingles sparked along my nerve endings.

Like magic, the rest of our clothes were off and flung across the tent. Our sweat-slick skin slid together until his hardness found the wetness between my thighs. Heat engulfed me as he thrust inside. Warmth built with each glide back and forth, until molten heat filled me. My legs tightened around him. I never wanted to let go.

Our groans filled the tent as we came together. He collapsed on top of me for a second, before he turned to fall on the mattress, keeping his arms about me. We snuggled as a breeze found its way through the mesh window at the back of the tent. It faced away from everyone, so I could leave it open for air and light.

His fingers tangled in my hair as he swept it back from my eyes. He gazed at me and I saw something other than satisfied lust in his eyes. His next words confirmed it.

"I could stay right here forever."

I swallowed deeply, dryness coating my throat. Thinking the same thought was not like saying it aloud. "There is no more forever. Not anymore. You know that, right?" My heartbeat was racing, thumping hard in my temples. "We don't even know if there will be a tomorrow."

His hand slid down and cupped my cheek. "There will always be a tomorrow. The sun will rise. The sun will set. The Earth will go on spinning."

I tried for lightness. "The sun could go supernova or something. Like they used to show on those Discovery Channel programs." My voice hitched to a stop as the twinkle left his extraordinary greenish-brown eyes.

He grabbed my hands, massaging my fingers. "Don't do that, Em. This isn't about me getting my rocks off. You are more than that."

I pulled my hands back and covered my breasts with a blanket. "I don't want this to mean more than that. Just sex. Can't you understand that? There is no future. Not for us. Not for the world. Not for anyone."

Seth moved closer until I had to stop or fall off the mattress onto the rooftop. His fingers grazed my chin and raised my face. The warmth had returned to his eyes.

"There used to be a saying when I was younger. There are girls you fuck and there are girls you marry. You, Emily Gray, are not one of those just for fucking."

He laughed; his head thrown back and a twinkle in his eyes. "You should see your face. I'm not proposing marriage or anything close. But you are better than a one-night or several nights stand. You are special, Emily and I'd like to be with you until one of us doesn't want to be. Can you do that?"

I dropped the blanket and launched myself at him. We fell backward on the mattress. Tears filled my eyes and dripped onto Seth's face. "Yes, yes, a thousand times yes."

◆ ◆ ◆

Dawn broke and the sun rose over the Streets of Brentwood. Commander Jack Canida rubbed the tiredness from his eyes. He hadn't gone to sleep yet. The news continued to filter in from Concord Hospital and Jed Long, the ham radio operator there. Survivor camps were continuing to fall all over Concord and Pleasant Hill. One by one, they were calling for help over the static-filled airwaves, and then falling silent. Jed mentioned the squeal on the radio from each location but damned if Jack knew what it all meant. His MOS in the army had been artillery, not communications.

He looked up when Paul Luther entered the communications trailer. A nod and he turned back to where Beth was delicately turning knobs to find one of the small communities they talked to each week for an update.

"Sunvalley, come in. This is Streets of Brentwood. Sunvalley, are you there?"

Jack's fists tightened at his sides. The Sunvalley group was bigger than their own. Over five hundred people were using the mall roofs of the shopping center in the heart of Pleasant Hill. He'd visited there once in the early days to set up communications between the groups.

"Streets of Brent—wood. This is Sun—ey.

You're breaking up. We are having trouble reaching several groups here. College Park is off the dial. Nothing but that low hum we are getting all over the airwaves."

"Sunvalley. Please describe the hum."

"Streets group, it is a low-level squeal. Comes and goes on the dial. High-pitched. Sets my fillings to aching," the voice laughed.

Jack looked to Paul who just shrugged. He leaned over Beth's shoulder. "Try to get the College Park group."

She turned the dials to the setting on her piece of paper. Nothing there, but the static and the low hum. Beth rubbed her cheek with the heel of her hand.

"It does make your fillings ache. I've only got the one, but it's like biting a fork when you eat." She shuddered. "I hate that."

"Keep trying, Beth. Go down the list and mark who you reach and who you don't."

He tapped Paul's arm and jerked his head. They both stepped outside of the trailer. The stairs creaked with their weight. Jack moved away from the trailer and Paul followed.

"I don't know what to think. Do you think we're seeing an influx from somewhere else? Walnut Creek, or further out, Danville maybe?"

Paul scratched his chin. "The groups have been reporting low numbers of zombs. A small group here and there, same as we are. Nothing like a horde big enough to take on a well-armed group of live humans. You think they got out of San Fran? Swam across?" Paul laughed and stopped abruptly as if at the thought of zombies being able to swim.

Jack shuddered, a chill running up his spine. "Swimmers? Damn, that is all we need. They'll be floating down the San Joaquin and running over Antioch in no time." *If a whale could do it, why not zombies?*

He stared north, as if he could see through the buildings, across the short distance to the river north of Antioch. He ran numbers in his head. Only a little more than ten miles by car separated Brentwood from the river. If the creatures got out of downtown Antioch and hit Highway 4, they could be in Brentwood in a couple of hours, even shambling along.

"We need someone to run recon by the river." Jack turned to Paul. "Do you think the way is open enough for Seth and his truck?"

Paul stared over his shoulder. He turned. "Speak of the devil," Jack whispered.

Goose bumps rose up on his arms. Like someone stepping on his grave, his mother would have said when he was little. Seth stared at Commander Canida and his buddy, Paul. They had grim smiles on their faces that promised anything but a happy day.

Sweat formed on his hand, the one holding Emily's. He tried to pull away and she gave his fingers a firm squeeze and held on tighter. Tension seized his shoulders. As if his mother knew what he'd been doing with Emily. He stood taller and strode to the men's side.

"What can I do for you gentlemen?"

Paul stepped back and Jack slid his hands to his back and assumed parade rest.

This was official Streets of Brentwood business. He took a deep breath and relaxed. *Has nothing to do with Emily and me.*

Jack coughed and cleared his throat. "We need you to drive down to the river in Antioch and see if we have a problem with floaters or swimmers. This isn't an order, just a request. But we think you have the best chance of making it with your truck since you make runs all over the area."

"And I'm not a member here, so I'm expendable?"

The commander stepped back as if Seth had yelled instead of the soft voice he'd used. "I'm sorry, Jack. That was uncalled for. Of course, I'll check out the river for you. Anything else?"

"Yeah, Seth. I'm sorry, but we really need you to run to the Concord Hospital. We're hearing some disturbing things."

Emily spoke up. "Do you need me to leave?"

Seth pulled her to his side. "No. I'm sure this concerns all of us."

Jack nodded. "It does. I don't want this spread about yet, but the camps and groups in Concord are falling off the grid. Communications are going black. The people at the hospital are vulnerable. I don't need to tell you that, Seth."

No, he didn't need to be told that. His mother was there, oblivious in her coma. With one arm, he squeezed Emily closer to his side.

"I'll check out the river, check in, and then I'll head to the Concord Hospital. I'll take Emily with me."

She jerked away from his side. "Excuse me. You'll take me with you? Whether I want to go with you or not?"

Jack and Paul coughed and looked away. "I'll leave you two to it. Just let me know when you're leaving so we can discuss radio frequencies," Jack added and the two men walked away.

He looked at Emily. "I'm sorry. I should have asked if you wanted to go. I figured it didn't matter if you stayed, anyone can do your job, and you could get away for a while."

If anything, her look had gone from angry to pissed off in the second it took to get out his sentence. *What did I say?* He ran his fingers through his hair and fiddled with his lucky shamrock earring.

"I don't need to get away for a while," she threw his words back at him. "This is my home now. I have a job to put down zombies and I do it damned well. I'm not some arm candy to make you look good, Carl."

Her cheeks flashed bright red and she looked away. "I don't know where that came from. I'm so sorry."

Seth stepped closer, caressing her shoulders.

"I'm not your husband. I just thought you might like to go somewhere else for a while. Spend some more time together. Guess I was wrong."

Her head came up and her eyes flooded with tears. "I guess you were," she whispered, pulling back out of reach.

He shrugged. "I'll get my stuff and get out of your way, then."

Not looking back, he left her standing there.

CHAPTER ELEVEN

I looked, and there before me was a pale horse! Its rider was named Death, and Hades was following close behind him.
— Revelation 6:8 King James Bible

Concord Hospital
Concord, California

General Martin Peters rode in the reinforced Jeep, the behemoth of an armored school bus casting a shadow over the smaller vehicle. Speakers mounted on the bus's roof broadcast the drone signal. The sound had numbed his teeth miles ago. The high-pitched whistle barely noticeable after the hours spent listening to it except for the incessant throb at the base of his skull. He'd have a headache tonight. But it would all be worth it.

They'd rounded up the undead as they traveled. Captain Gomez set the signal to repel the horde before them, rolling along slow enough so they didn't run over the slowest shambling creature. A journey that in the past would have taken an hour, maybe, now consisted of most of the day to travel a simple twenty-five miles.

Martin cracked his neck, moving in his seat to get the kinks out of his back. They'd spent last night on the freeway, just before the city limits. Antonio set the speakers to a tone that put the zombies into a swaying stupor, and he and his men slept like babies for the first time in a long time.

He wanted to hit the hospital in daylight. He wanted the people to see him coming. He wanted them to know he was King of the Zombie Horde.

They'd hit the mall last, hitting a small strip

mall and a community college first to see how it went. It had gone like clockwork. The zombies swayed in their stupor and his crew fitted them with suicide bomber vests. He growled. *The only good thing to come out of the years of the war on terror was thinking like the terrorists. And you didn't even have to promise these guys seventy-two virgins.*

Not since the plane crash of '85 had the mall sustained such damage. The zombies piled on each other against the walls, pressing the front row into the cement barrier. Martin had pushed the detonator button and laughed as rotting body parts and bloody debris rained down on the parking lot. The whistle drove the zombies further and further into the building like lemmings off a cliff. More explosions rang out and the roof collapsed, taking zombies and humans with it. His men shot anything left moving, stumbling out of the debris dust cloud.

Now they sat up the road from the hospital. He got out of the Jeep and stared at the sun. They had a few hours until sunset. Plenty of time to take the hospital, get a few doctors or nurses for the compound, and all the drugs and medical supplies they could carry.

Antonio walked to his side with Tanya in tow. His fingers itched to touch her. He fisted his hands at his sides as the man started talking and his wife hung onto his arm. He pushed down the growl in his throat. The bitch knew exactly what she was doing. Her smug smile said it all. She thought she could have her husband and string him along on the side. No damned way. Antonio was going to have an unfortunate accident as soon as his usefulness died. When it happened, he'd make the bitch watch. He'd take her right there, before her husband's corpse turned cold, or turned undead. He hadn't decided which yet.

He grabbed the binoculars Antonio held out and scanned the building.

"The western wall would be the easiest to breach. Looks like offices and stuff. It's the one with the Dumpsters parked up against it."

"I know which way is west," he huffed, with a quick glance to the sun.

He stared through the binoculars. "I only want to take out a small section. Then we send in the creatures on fire and have the whole hospital in a panic. We might lose some, but we'll round up most of them and sort out who we need and kill the rest."

"Just because they aren't doctors or nurses, doesn't mean we don't need their skills," Antonio stuttered. "There could be cooks, repairmen, or someone we need. We've lost many men to the zombies."

Martin lowered the binoculars and glared at his captain. "I don't need to explain myself to you. All you have to do is follow orders. We have too many mouths to feed now as it is. Inventory says we have three months tops before we start rationing or starving. This trip has been to see if we could take something as big as a mall. After that demonstration at Sun Valley we should take this hospital like a walk in the park. Then we strike at The Streets of Brentwood group. That location is an over-ripe plum waiting to fall in our hands. Along with everything else Brentwood has, food, water, and women, we'll be sitting pretty when winter comes."

Tanya glared at him out of her husband's line of sight. He'd known that last remark about women would get to her. He had orders for the woman as well. "Mrs. Gomez, I want you to be in charge of Miranda."

He pulled a leash from his pocket and handed it to Tanya. "Stay close to the bus and keep an eye on her. She's been trying to run away lately, and I'll want her later."

Tanya snatched the leash out of his hand and stomped off. Beside him, Antonio cleared his throat. "Don't say a word. You could still work your machine minus a tongue. We all have our jobs to do. Miranda's is to keep me happy. Yours is to direct the horde. Let's get to it."

Antonio did his job well, albeit with shaking hands. Martin smiled. *Good, remember who is in charge here.* He stood beside his captain, keeping one eye on the control board and the other on the advancing horde.

Row after row of undead advanced on the hospital. Their nonexistent perimeter of piles of dirt and cement blocks fell in mere minutes. The few outlying guards were overwhelmed by rotting flesh, and then turned quickly to join the horde. They doubled their numbers in minutes.

He stared as a man had his arms ripped off,

only to rise a moment later to shamble in the direction of the building. All this power was his. He would own all of California before next summer. Straightening his spine, he jammed his hands on his hips. Hell, the whole North American continent could be his.

Explosions rocked the area as the first wave reached the wall. More and more undead piled against the cracking wall until it collapsed, taking the first group with it.

"The fire zombies next," he ordered Gomez.

The man's fingers danced over the controls and the horde stood still yards from the fallen wall. Peters' men rushed forward with torches and lit up the swaying zombies. Antonio's fingers flew to set the undead, now aflame, moving toward and then inside the hospital.

Panicked screams rose above the moans of the undead menace. Martin bounced on the balls of his feet. Soon! He glanced at his watch and returned his gaze to the hospital. Flames crackled as curtains flared on fire. Live people streamed out the doors, clothes on fire. They fell to the ground with whimpers. The creatures fell upon them and soon they rose to join their undead brethren.

He lifted the bullhorn. "This is General Peters. Surrender and you may live. Resist and you all die." Faces appeared at the windows on the upper floors. "You have minutes to live before the zombies reach you."

Clicking off the bullhorn, Martin turned to

Antonio. "Make them stand still so the men can move in."

Antonio did his stuff and the undead stopped in their tracks, swaying to music only they could hear. Martin waved his arm and the men moved in. Screams erupted from the building. He smiled. The zombies were still not moving. His men were having their fun. He would give them a couple of minutes, and then he was going in to pick who lived and who died.

♦♦♦

Jed Long's fingers twisted the knobs on the ham radio. Nothing came in except for the barely audible screech on all frequencies. A few moments ago, an explosion had rocked the building. Plaster dust had fallen on his head and the radio. He'd looked outside to see hundreds of rotting undead swarming the hospital, more than he'd seen since the Z virus struck months ago. The far western end of the building collapsed on the horde.

The pieces were falling into place. He rushed to the window again and gazed down on an army of zombies just standing in place. His ham radio hummed. Grabbing a recorder, he held it to the speaker and pushed the record button.

The smell of smoke wafted up to his room just as the door slammed open, hitting the wall behind, and slamming shut again. Dr. Shannon Drake stood there, gasping for breath, tears running down her face. Screams echoed through the hospital.

"Jed, we have to get out of here now. There's an army outside, and I don't mean the zombie one. It's as if they can control them and make them do what they want. Some maniac who is calling himself General Peters seems to be in charge. The hospital is lost. We have nothing to fight them with and there are just too many. We have to get to Brentwood and Commander Canida. He has the weapons and the numbers to put up a fight."

They both jumped as the door opened again. Jed shoved Shannon behind him. Amy stepped through the door. Her clothes were ripped and a nasty scratch ran down her face and neck. Blood oozed from it.

She gasped for breath and leaned back against the closed door. "There're coming. They're looking for doctors and nurses and killing the rest." Gunshots and screams from the floor below punctuated her words.

Jed turned to look at his equipment on the desk. Both women grabbed an arm. "We can't take it with us, Jed," Shannon said, moving the group toward the window.

She opened it and looked down. "There's no one in the back. We are out of here. We'll take the fire escape and hide out until dark."

Amy and Jed quickly straddled the windowsill and climbed out onto the fire escape. Shannon stood in the room, her head twisting back and forth from them and the door.

Amy grabbed her hand. "Don't even think

about it. We can't save the patients. We have to let Canida know what he's facing. One of the soldiers bragged to another that the Streets of Brentwood was next so they would be comfortable this winter."

"Doc, grab my gun. It's under the mattress," Jed said, leaning in the window.

Shannon grabbed the weapon and pulled herself through the window. The trio looked down. Still no one. They climbed down and sprinted for the nearby tree-covered walking path.

Finding a giant, straggly bush, they hunkered down and stared at the destruction. Shannon whispered to the others. "I don't get it. Why didn't they surround the building?"

They saw a few others escape as they had, but they were too far away to call out. Amy whispered back. "I don't think they are real soldiers, even if that guy did say he was General Peters. They seemed unorganized, letting the zombies do all the work."

Shannon stood up. "Let's find somewhere to hide until morning. Then we try to find a car and get to Brentwood."

◆◆◆

Miranda Stevens had had it. She was neck-deep in shit and she wasn't taking it anymore. The collar and leash were humiliating enough, but having Tanya Gomez at the other end of the rope was too much.

It wouldn't be so bad if the woman just stood there, but she wouldn't shut up. Every remark out of her mouth was designed to cut and wound. She knew Tanya was sleeping with Peters. A shudder ripped through her. *Why would anyone willingly have sex with that dirty old man?*

Mrs. Gomez outweighed her by a good thirty pounds and she had some muscle beneath that fat. The slaps hurt, but no more than the ones she got every day from Peters. The pinches annoyed as she tried to move away, only to be brought up short by the leash. She'd tried to get the collar off while she'd been alone in the bus, but it had a lock and Martin had the key.

No, what hurt the most was watching Tanya brush her long, thick hair, and then reach over and run a hand over Miranda's shaved head. In her nineteen years it had never even been cut, until Martin had a fit when she refused certain kinky sexual acts. He'd beat her unconscious and taken hair clippers to her head. She'd come to in agony and bald.

She flinched as Tanya ran a hand over her head again. She tried to scrunch up her shoulders but the woman just pulled tighter on the leash until Miranda was practically in her lap.

"I can see why Martin keeps you like this. It's kind of like having a pet." Fingers trailed down her shoulder to her barely-covered breast. They tweaked her nipple.

Miranda exploded. She may be forced to be Peters' sex slave, but she had had enough. She turned around and sank her teeth into Tanya's hand. The woman screeched, reared back, and slapped Miranda full-force across the face.

She fell to the floor and the woman leapt on top of her, her fingers wrapping around her neck. Spots appeared before her eyes, and she tried to breathe. No air. Her body jerked, trying to get the woman off her.

With her last drop of energy, she brought her feet up, wrapped them around Tanya's neck, and slammed her head into the bus floor. A crack echoed as Miranda sat up, catching her breath.

Mrs. Gomez lay at her feet, just the bare movement of her chest showing she was still alive. Blood pooled behind her head. Miranda eased the leash out of Tanya's hand and unclipped it from the collar.

Still, the woman didn't move. Miranda turned her head and glanced out the windows of the bus. No soldiers. No zombs. No one. For the first time in weeks, she was alone.

Spotting some camo shirts and pants, she pulled them on over the lacy bra and panties; the only clothing Martin let her wear. She grabbed a cap and pulled it on over her shorn head. All the boots were many sizes too big, so she tiptoed past Gomez and slowly slid the door open and stepped outside.

She took a deep breath. Free! She glanced at the burning hospital lighting up the twilight and turned in the opposite direction, melting into the deepening gloom.

CHAPTER TWELVE

Everything I am as a man;
I learned from my mother.
Everything I am as a person;
I learned from my mother.
Everything I am,
I am because of my mother.
— Seth Ripley

Night fell as Seth came over the rise of the road just before the hospital. Death, destruction, and fire greeted him. He slammed on the brakes and turned off the truck with a hard twist of the keys. What had started out as a few hours, maybe half a day drive to Concord, had become a nightmare of two days on the road.

The drive to the Antioch riverfront had taken longer than expected, but not because of danger, just lots of disabled cars filled the streets. Every path stopped him dead in his tracks, forced to back up and find another way. One detour led to another, until he wished for the good old days of GPS. He would have even welcomed the robotic female voice telling him 'Recalculating.' He'd been forced to use landmarks and the sun's position to find his way north to the river.

Once he faced the San Joaquin River, he scanned the area and spotted nothing. He radioed in to Canida and let him know he was moving on to the hospital. What should have taken a few hours dragged on as he used the push bar on his truck to clear wreck after wreck. The metal-scraping sound settled a pounding in his head. Uncountable numbers of undead flooded the road as well. He'd seen nothing at the river, but the freeway was packed. They all seemed to be marching west toward Concord. Good news for the Streets of Brentwood group, but not for the hospital and those few souls left in Concord.

Night had fallen and forced him to sleep on

the road in his truck. With the number of shambling undead, he climbed on top of the trailer and stretched out to sleep. He lay back on the warm metal and watched the stars in a clear sky. No light pollution, no pollution period. The sky had probably not been this clear since before the Gold Rush. The Milky Way streamed across the sky. He could pick out Perseus, Cassiopeia, and Pegasus no problem at all.

Years ago, in rural Woodland, Uncle John had taken him and his cousins out to a pasture with a telescope to point out the planets and constellations. He sighed. Were Uncle John, Aunt Jen, and the cousins, Ben and Becky even still alive? He closed his eyes to the rhythmic moaning and shuffling on the road below. *Go away. Just go away.*

The next day had been more of the same, until long past dark he'd reached the hospital. All the hallmarks of a devastating battle shone in the weak moonlight. Dead bodies littered the road as far as he could see. Part of the hospital had collapsed into a pile of rubble, and fires flickered in the shattered windows. Like a news broadcast from the war-torn countries of Iraq or Afghanistan.

His heart beat against his ribcage. The doctors and nurses had had no way to move the patients. Some couldn't be moved at all. He lowered his head and uttered a prayer. "Please let my mother have gone in her sleep. Let her soul be at rest."

He crossed himself and jumped down from the truck.

Nothing moved as he ran to the building. Still, he didn't yell. His throat was dry. He probably couldn't yell, even if he'd tried. The doors were blasted off their hinges, on the ground or barely hanging on with scraps of twisted metal. His steps crunched in the eerie silence as he walked over broken glass.

The bodies of men and children filled the corridor. Bullet holes in the foreheads told the story. This hadn't been a zombie horde, or at least not just the horde, as he spotted burnt bodies among the other dead.

Farther down the hallway, he saw older women and invalid patients shot in their wheelchairs and on their gurneys. Bile rose in his throat. He refused to release it and further foul the dead. Swallowing hard, he moved onward. Silent prayers clouded his head.

He examined every female body, but none was his mother. He found a stairway and started up. Carla's room had been on the second floor. No dead or undead littered the upstairs floor. The smoke was heavier up here, as if a fire still raged in the building, although he spotted no flames or heard any crackling sounds.

When he reached her room, he stopped at the door, his hand resting on the handle. *Did he really need to see her? Did he need to see if fire or the undead had taken her?*

Taking a dead breath and holding it, he pushed the door open. It stopped after a couple of inches. He looked down and wished he hadn't. Charred flesh covered a gnawed leg. He assumed it was attached to a body, since the door was stuck.

"Son of a bitch," he whispered. Leaning his shoulder against the door, he pushed until the body gave way. He fell into the room. His mind fought to comprehend what his eyes saw. A group of the undead surrounded his mother's bed. The unmistakable sound of them feeding was the last straw. His stomach rebelled and he lost its contents all over the floor.

Like hyenas spotting a fresh meal, they all looked up at once. Blood and gore dripped from their mouths as they started shambling his way. Their moans raised the hair on his neck.

A quick glance across the room showed a man—or what was left of one on the bed. He caught his breath and gagged on the rancid stench. His gaze shot right and left, trying to spot anything to use against them. They were moving in too close for him to reach his gun.

He lunged for the IV stand and used its metal feet to push the group away. They stumbled and fell over each other. Seth ripped the stand apart, throwing the bottom half against the wall. Grabbing the top, he turned it around and used it as a sword. He plunged it into the eye socket of an older man, and pulled it out in time to stab a young woman in the throat.

Both went down with a wet thud, and stayed down.

A hand grabbed his foot. The body on the

floor moved. He pulled his gun and shot the thing.

He whipped around at a scraping noise on the floor. The abomination coming toward him shouldn't exist. The burned flesh had fallen off most of its body. In places, he could see through the creature to the other side of the room. He said a prayer and shot it in the head. It hit the floor with a sound like falling pins in a bowling alley.

Shuddering, he looked up as the last one reached him.

He looked into hazel-colored eyes that matched his own, except covered with a milky film.

His heart stopped.

"Mama," he cried, his voice breaking like a teenager's.

The gun shook in his hand as he placed the barrel against her forehead. His finger trembled on the trigger. His vision blurred with tears raining down his face. A thousand priceless memories ripped through his mind in a split-second. Of this woman holding him, kissing his skinned knees, and being there every moment of his life.

The moment of inattention cost him. Bloody hands grabbed the gun and the hand holding it. Teeth sunk deep into his flesh. A scream echoed in the room. It took a second to realize it was his own.

"Why?" he yelled, pulling his hand back and flinging her body across the room. He cradled his arm and bleeding hand as his mother's body connected with the wall. The sound of her neck breaking reached him as he slid down the door and plopped to the floor at the same time she did.

"Mama," he cried like when he was a child and had a nightmare. Only his mother couldn't chase the monster away; she was the monster. Or maybe he was the monster and there was no escaping himself and what he'd done.

He raised the gun to his face. *It would be so easy to end it now. Do it. No more of this shit. Just check out.*

The gun chattered against his teeth as he placed the barrel in his mouth. It tasted of metal and oil and death. His thumb pressed on the trigger. He pressed harder. A moan sounded from the bed.

He ripped the gun from his mouth, scraping his teeth in the process. Marching over to the bed, he put the gun up against the man's forehead and pulled the trigger. He put the gun back in the holster on his belt.

"One death in the family is enough for today."

With care, he squatted down and scooped his mother into his arms. She weighed nothing. Her illness and coma had stolen the solid shape of the woman he remembered from childhood. He left the room behind and moved down a deserted hallway to the stairs. He whispered the Twenty-third Psalm as he took the stairs one at a time.

By the time he reached the ground floor, the sweat was dripping off him in buckets. His mother's weight had increased a hundredfold and still it wasn't as heavy as his heart. His whispering stopped as he pushed open the door to the outside.

"...and I will dwell in the house of the Lord forever."

His knees refused to hold him any longer. He fell to the ground, his mother slipping from his slick, wet arms. He tried to open his eyes. His hand throbbed with every heartbeat. The scent of blood filled his nostrils and cramped his belly. It smelled so good.

A shadow passed between the moonlight and his eyelids. He squinted. A young soldier stood over him.

"Mr. Ripley?"

He prayed it didn't hurt to die.

He prayed that Heaven wasn't a lie.

He prayed the young man did it right and he didn't come back.

◆◆◆

Miranda Stevens stood over a man she was sure was Seth Ripley, the truck driver. She'd had a crush on him, just like every woman, young or old, when he'd deliver supplies to the compound. She stared at the woman he'd dropped. Hazel eyes staring straight ahead, she may be a relative. The woman seemed old enough to be his mother, with gray in her hair and wrinkles around her mouth.

His mumblings drew her attention back to him, something about making it quick and painless. She spotted his bitten hand and drew in a gasp. Her shoulders slumped. He was as good as dead.

She tried to turn away but he grabbed her

ankle. Tugging did nothing; the man had a vise grip on her.

"Let me go," she gritted out.

His eyes opened. "Please."

She sighed as he passed out and his hand dropped from her ankle. She should leave now and try to find others. Some people may have escaped the hospital. Not everyone had to be as evil as Martin Peters. Or the monsters at the compound, who'd followed Peters' lead and treated women like whores and toys to discard when they were done with them.

Just go. He's going to die anyway. And then rise up. Better to be far gone when that happens.

She couldn't. It was that 'please.' Her memories of his nice treatment of everyone when he'd come to the compound and brightened everyone's day. Sometimes, he came with footballs for the boys and toys for the little ones. Occasionally, he'd bring a doll or two for the little girls. Not necessities, but treasures of what was gone, that he'd risked his life to find and bring to them. He'd done it with no thought of gain, just because it was his nature to be kind.

Looking around, she spotted a wheelbarrow. Probably used to haul the sandbags they'd used for useless barricades. She pulled it over and after a lot of huffing and puffing and moaning and groaning, on both their parts, she got Seth into the thing.

She pulled his gun out of the holster and laid it on his chest for easy access. Turning to what was surely his mother, she debated with herself what to do. He'd obviously carried her outside for a reason. Most likely, to bury her with respect. She put her hands on her back and bent backward, groaning as it popped. She could get Seth somewhere safe, maybe, or bury his mother, but she wasn't managing both on her own.

Miranda moved to the woman's side. She straightened out the legs and moved her bent neck so it was where it belonged. Then, she moved sandbags until the woman was covered.

"Sorry, Seth. That's the best I can do."

The man's mumblings were building in volume until Miranda stopped and crammed her cap into his mouth. The wheelbarrow gathered weight as they traveled, harder to push with each step. Her stops became more frequent as her sweaty hands slipped off the handles.

After what seemed like the hundredth time, she took a break and gazed around. Still no zombies in their area, although their moans echoed across the empty streets. She shivered. They had to get inside. Somewhere.

A glimmer shined in the corner of her eye. She turned and spotted an intact window, a surprise all its own. The word Pharmacy written across it was like a sign from above, if she still believed in all that crap.

She grabbed the gun off the man's chest and pushed through the door. Taking a deep breath, she tasted dust and not much else.

"Hello," she whispered. Nothing.

She spotted a stairway in the back. With the gun pointed in front of her, she made her way up the stairs to an apartment. Tapping on each door raised no sounds at all. Going into each room, she made sure it was empty and moved on, shutting doors behind her. No zombie was sneaking up on her.

Not believing her good luck, she spoke louder. "Anyone home?"

Still nothing.

Miranda rushed down the stairs to get Seth.

Seth started thrashing around in the wheelbarrow, threatening to overturn it. She grabbed a hold of the handles and held it still.

With limited options, she dumped the wheelbarrow over and Seth to the ground. He moaned slightly, the cap still in his mouth. Moving inches at a time, with her hands under his arms, she got the man through the door, across the floor, and to the stairs.

A few steps. Take a break.

A few steps. Take a break.

With the sunrise peeking through tattered curtains, Miranda finally pulled Seth into the empty apartment. She got him tied to an enormous oak dining-room table with curtains ripped from the windows before she collapsed on the floor a safe distance away.

CHAPTER THIRTEEN

Shannon Drake sat up as the sun came through a tattered curtain hanging half off the rod and flooded the empty room. Jed and Amy were tangled around each other across the space. The young nurse was moaning and struggling in Jed's arms.

She jumped up and rushed to the young man's side. Amy's eyes were glazed over with a death haze. Her teeth snapped closer and closer to Jed's arms.

"Please, Amy. Stop." His pleas fell on dead ears. The woman's struggles grew stronger as Jed started crying and appeared to have given up.

With her added height and weight, Shannon grabbed the girl by the shoulders and flung her across the room. The thing rushed back across the space to meet the doctor's foot to her stomach. They both heard the crack as Amy's head connected with the windowsill. Jed winced, but Shannon didn't have time as the girl came at her again. This time she met her with a headlock. She twisted her arms, a loud crack sounded in the silence, and Amy's slight body fell to the dirty floor.

"But it was only a scratch. She was fine when we went to sleep," Jed's confused voice echoed in the now quiet room.

"It must have been enough. So close to her carotid artery, it probably just traveled that much faster through her system," Shannon provided, using medical jargon to distance herself from the senseless death of someone who had been her friend.

She turned away and gathered the knapsack and some belongings they had collected on their way to this apartment building. Jed grabbed her arm and spun her around.

"We can't just leave her like that. Or is she just another dead body to you? Do you see so many as a doctor that they just aren't people anymore?"

Grabbing his hand, she pried his fingers off, and then held them. "That isn't fair. Amy was a friend. A good friend. But this is the world we live in now. We can't risk burying her. We won't have time. Those are the facts."

He pulled away from her. "We can at least wrap her up. At least say good-bye."

Dropping the knapsack, she hugged him. He fought at first, until his sobs grew and he held on to her like his anchor in a storm. "Yes, we can do that," she whispered.

Jed got a clean blanket from a closet, while Shannon straightened Amy's broken neck and arranged her arms and legs. Together, they rolled her in the blanket and then sat on the floor, one on each side.

Shannon took off her lab coat and placed it over Amy's body. Jed removed the Star of David necklace he wore, pulling it over his head. She watched as the young man lifted Amy and put it on her. They bowed their heads, but she was out of prayers for any of them. If God was there, he wasn't listening.

Finally, they gathered their stuff and left the apartment, shutting the door silently behind them. Jed pulled a marker out of his pocket and scrawled Amy across the beige paint. His hand shook. "Shit, I don't even know her last name."

He looked at the floor but she still caught a glimpse of his red, flushed cheeks.

"Johannson," Shannon whispered.

He wrote it with a shaking hand and added September 21, 0 AZ below her name.

"AZ?"

"After the Z virus," Jed said, tucking the marker into his pocket.

The trip down the stairs passed in silence, Shannon listening for the undead and Jed lost in his misery, arms wrapped around his stomach. Nothing came at them from any of the apartments. She pushed open the glass doors in the entryway. The silence in the streets was overpowering. People can get used to anything over time, and six months of shuffling feet, moans at all hours, and the screams of the dying can become just background noise, like cars, airplanes, and kids playing had been before.

The sun was halfway to noon and no birdsong filled the air. No voices broke the quiet. No moans sent them running. Shannon's head whipped back and forth, waiting for the expected horde to appear. Nothing.

"Maybe they all died in the hospital attack?" Jed questioned.

"Maybe. But that's a lot of zombies to just be gone."

"Maybe the general took them with him?"

"What did you say?" Shannon whispered back, afraid to tempt fate by speaking any louder.

"He can control the zombies."

"What?" she asked back just a little too loud.

A moan echoed from around the side of the building. An old man stumbled into view. He was more skeletal remains than a person. His clothes held what was left of him together. The stench reached them before he did.

Jed dropped his pack and started rummaging through it. Shannon grabbed his shoulder. "Not now, we have to go."

He pulled away. "This will only take a minute."

She searched the area. The walking undead guy appeared to be alone; no friends joined it yet. Out of the corner of her eye, she spotted bright blue in the road. A semi truck with a trailer sat not a hundred yards away. Turning back to tell Jed, she stopped speaking in the middle of talking. The sight in front of her was unfathomable.

The young man held a voice recorder in his hand. She couldn't tell if it were on but it must be because the abomination stopped shuffling along and stood in place, swaying to music only it seemed able to hear, his head turned up to the sky.

"We need to go now," she whispered, yanking on Jed's shoulder. "We have to let the people in Brentwood know."

Slowly, she stepped backward, turning to check for obstacles, gazing in morbid wonder at the unmoving zombie. After what seemed a century, her back hit the truck's bumper. She let go of Jed and slid along it to the door. Seth Ripley was painted across it in bright white lettering. Shannon gazed right and left but she didn't see the truck driver anywhere. Her heart thundered in her chest with the memory of leaving Carla Ripley, along with the other patients, at the hospital.

Climbing up, she pulled the door open and slid inside. The keys were in the ignition but Seth was not in the truck as she risked a quick backward glance to the sleeper. From her higher vantage point, she stared as far as she could see, but nothing.

The other door opened and Jed climbed in. "Where's Ripley?"

"He's not here. But the truck is. I can't turn this thing around so we'll have to take back roads to Brentwood and hope the general's having problems on the freeway. We have to get that recording to the Brentwood group."

♦♦♦

Walking back from the communications trailer, I chewed on my nails. Three days and we'd still had no word from Seth. Nothing after he'd left the river and headed to the hospital. The hospital had gone silent too and the looks shooting back and forth from Canida and Luther had the hair standing up on the back of my neck and my nails bitten down to the quick. The tension in the trailer had been thick enough to choke my breathing.

I'd been berating myself for days. Why had I let Seth leave with anger between us? When I wasn't chastising myself, Michelle was doing it for me. All I wanted was to see him again and apologize. Life was too short to let arguments get between relationships. We should have talked, but he'd walked away so fast and I'd waited too long to try to call him back.

Feminine voices called my name. I took a few more steps before it registered that Michelle and Bobbie were calling me over. A small group of ladies were gathered at the edge of the garden. Several women seemed to be taking a break and leaning on hoes and rakes.

Michelle rushed over, linked arms, and dragged me to the group. Looking around, I saw several faces I vaguely knew. These were the women who keep us fed, and the camp running, while I'd been out shooting zombs and getting supplies.

"Anything?" Bobbie asked.

"Nothing," I whispered, my voice catching. "Nothing from Concord at all. It's as if the town is gone. I don't know how big it was, but they're not getting anyone on the radio."

"About a hundred, maybe hundred twenty thousand. Before..." a small, very pregnant woman provided before her voice trailed off and tears gathered in her eyes.

Michelle moved to the young woman's side and gave her a hug and a shoulder to cry on.

A truck's air horn sounded from outside the mall. My head whipped around as the cargo containers rose and a dark-blue semi rolled inside. My heart stopped and then raced wildly.

"Seth," I whispered. My gaze swept the truck, but the only people were a blonde woman and a man with long hair and glasses on the seat beside her.

"It's okay. He's in the back with the patients," I murmured, a cold chill sweeping over my body as the truck pulled up to the communications trailer.

My feet were frozen to the ground as Canida and Luther pounded down the stairs and rushed to the truck. Jack hopped up and pulled the door open and the blonde tumbled out into his arms. The young man opened his door and ran around the front of the truck. I heard excited yelling, but the words are scrambled by the wind and the roaring in my ears.

I didn't know I'd taken the steps until I found myself at the vehicle. The guy was yelling at Paul Luther and playing some type of voice recorder for him. Jack Canida was kneeling on the ground, the blonde laying on the asphalt.

"Where's Seth?" I yelled. At least, I wanted to yell, but the words came out in a harsh whisper. "Where's Seth?"

The guy's head swung up, his blue eyes locked to mine. "We never saw him. Just the truck."

Two steps and I found myself in his face with handfuls of T-shirt in my grasp. "Did you look for him? Or did you just run away like a coward?"

Canida's gruff tones penetrated my anger, as he demanded I let go. I opened my hands and stepped back. The guy fell back against the truck's grill. He shook his head.

"He wasn't there. I swear. We looked."

My breath came in heavy pants. Wiping my hands on my jeans, I turned away. *Where was he? Where was Seth?* Searching my head and my heart, I find nothing. No pang. No grief. *He wasn't dead. I would know it. Wouldn't I?*

Michelle came up and wrapped me in a hug. I breathed deep of her strawberry-scented shampoo. The essence of my friend, sunshine and happiness, wrapped up in a bottle. She and that fragrance never failed to calm me.

"Commander Jack said the doctor and her friend have stuff to tell us. He's calling a group meeting at the theater. Adults only." Michelle's words brought me back to the present. Finally, we'd have some answers to what was going on out there.

With Michelle on one side and Bobbie on the

other, we made our way to the movie theater. The lingering scent of movie house popcorn had my salivary glands working overtime. Happy memories of Saturday afternoon matinees juxtaposed with the hell we lived in now.

We found seats near the front and waited as the rest of the adult members of our community filed in, shuffled down the rows, and found a seat.

Michelle whispered in my ear. I laughed. Some old habits don't die. No matter how old you are, you still whisper in a theater. "The blonde is a doctor from the Concord hospital. I think I heard the guy say his name was Jed."

"Shhh," came from Bobbie on Michelle's other side as Jack Canida jumped up on the stage in front of the screen. Paul Luther followed.

Jack put his hands up and the room hushed. "I called this meeting because we finally have some news from Concord. This is Dr. Shannon Drake and her friend, Jed Long. They just came in from over the hill with news for us."

Canida's face wore a look I hadn't seen before. Even at the height of clearing our section of town of the undead, Jack always had a look of optimism. Not anymore. Jack had aged in the short time he'd heard from the doctor to now.

I tried to swallow against the knot in my throat.

The woman stepped forward. "I'm Dr. Drake. Shannon, please. We…" She motioned to the guy I'd shoved against the truck. He looked like the stereotypical comic-book-store owner, long hair in a ponytail and glasses sliding down his nose. "Jed and I were at the Concord hospital. We escaped. Along with Amy..." Her voice trailed off as Jed wiped his eyes and put his glasses back on.

My gut told me this Amy had turned...and been put down. They had that look in their faces. The one people get when they have to kill someone they loved or cared about.

"We escaped from the attack."

Voices sprang up across the room. Jack raised his hands. "Let them finish. Hold your questions."

"We were attacked by a man calling himself General Peters. He didn't have a bunch of men." She looked over the crowd. "Probably less than you have here right now. What he did have was an army—an army of the undead."

"Right." Jim Evans stood up a few seats over, putting his hands on his hips. "You want us to believe he just told them to attack and they listened?"

Dr. Drake motioned Jed forward. "This is Jed Long. He's a ham radio operator. He'll explain it."

Jed stepped forward. "I'm sure some of you know that communications have been spotty this week. There's been a subsonic sound on the airwaves. I don't know how to truly explain it. Think of a dog whistle. We can't hear it, but dogs can. The signal on the airwaves is something the zombs can hear, but we can't. Not really."

He turned on the voice recorder in his hand

and turned the volume knob.

I didn't hear anything, but my fillings could. Rubbing my jaw, the pain stayed and wouldn't go away. Others must have felt it too. I heard hissing and people grabbed and rubbed their faces. Elderly Mr. Buster slapped a hand to his forehead and I remembered he had a steel plate there, a souvenir of the Iraqi War.

I heard the click of a button and it stopped.

"When this played at the hospital the zombs just stood there. Swaying to something only they could hear. The other guys, the live ones, could walk among them and nothing happened. They put vests on them. They made the zombs into suicide bombers. They took down the hospital in minutes. They killed almost everyone."

"Almost everyone?" Jack asked.

Jed stuttered. "They took the young women and some doctors. They had lab coats, I think they were doctors. Killed everyone else."

"When was this?"

Shannon spoke up. "We left a day and a half ago. We took the back roads so it took longer, but we didn't want to run into General Peters on the freeway. I was sure I wouldn't find you guys still here, but we had to take a chance to let you know what you'll face. General Peters' men said The Streets of Brentwood were next."

A cacophony of voices rose in the theater. Everyone wanted to know everything at once. Jack raised his hands again. "One at a time."

I half-listened as questions were asked and

answered. My mind was far outside the walls of this shopping center. Besides, I only had two questions and neither Shannon nor Jed could answer them. Where was Seth? And why wasn't this 'General' Peters, whoever he was, here yet?

CHAPTER FOURTEEN

Apartment 10B
Concord, California

Miranda Stevens' mind was a centrifuge on overdrive. Should she stay? Should she go? Was it better to go it alone? Or was it better to wait for Seth? It had taken most of a day to get Seth Ripley up ten flights of stairs in the apartment building next to the pharmacy. Height equaled safety, as far as she was concerned. All the apartment doors had been open as if an evacuation had taken place at some time. She'd found no one inside, but plenty of supplies. If they'd been forced to leave, the tenants had left in a rush. Cupboards overflowed with boxed and canned goodness.

A moan from the back bedroom drew her attention whipping back to the present. She stood up and went to the doorway. Seth writhed on the bed like a caged animal, his wrists and ankles tied to the bed. Had it been two days? No, maybe it was three—in any case, he hadn't turned. He'd soaked the sheets through and the acrid smell of sweat wafted through the whole place. She didn't dare open a window for ventilation with his yells and screams coming without notice.

She tugged off her cap and ran a hand over her buzzed hair. Grimacing, she yanked the cap back on. Her gaze swept to the man's injured hand. Blood crusted on the bandage wrapped around what was left of his hand. Miranda swallowed the bile in her throat. She'd thrown up enough when she'd amputated his pinky and ring finger to try to save his life. And the jury was still out on that. Maybe she'd done all that damage for nothing.

The stench of burnt flesh would never leave her. She leaned up against the doorjamb. It was what it was. The curling iron that ran on butane was all she could find in the drug store to cauterize the wound she'd made of his hand.

"Now we wait," she whispered in the empty silence of the dwelling, only broken by Seth's thrashing and whimpering.

"Mama," he cried from the bed.

She went over and brushed the greasy strands of hair back from his heated forehead. He was burning up. Getting a bottle of water from the nightstand, she forced some down his throat and poured some on a washrag she'd used to wipe him down.

"No Mama. I'm sorry, Seth. You just have me."

His eyes remained a beautiful hazel color every time she raised the lids to look. No glassy, opaque look—yet. She pulled down the sheet and ran the damp cloth across his chest. He was so beautiful, so young. At least compared to Peters. A shudder ran through her body as her fingers trailed down his chest with the washcloth. Dark hair covered his torso and ran straight down to the buckle on his pants. Her fingertips grazed his belt buckle and she jumped back with a hiss as if the metal had burned her. The man was incoherent. She wouldn't be any better than Peters or his men.

Flinging the cloth across the room, she covered her eyes and the sobs broke. She wouldn't be one of them. They hadn't changed her that much. They'd taken her innocence; she wouldn't let them have taken her beliefs and values.

"I won't. I'm not a monster."

Her fingers trembled as she pulled the sheet back up to his chin. "You have to live, Seth. I can't do this alone."

Time passed as the sun traveled from the living-room window in the morning, baked the small apartment through the day, and then sank on the horizon out the bedroom window. Miranda filled the time with checking on Seth, keeping him alive with sips of water every hour, and searching the building and nearby stores for supplies.

Each morning she rushed from the couch to find him still unconscious, but not turned. Each evening she said the prayers she'd thought she'd lost, begging God to see Seth through this. Three more days passed before his fever broke. She checked his hand as she cleaned it and bandaged it up again. The burn scars made her stomach clench, but there were no red or black streaks running from the mutilated flesh. Thank goodness for medical shows on television. She smiled at the thought of the television being good for something.

Getting Seth cleaned up and settled with more blankets, she decided to take a sponge bath herself. Grabbing two gallon-bottles of water, she headed to the bathroom. She stripped and stared at herself in the mirror. She couldn't do anything about her missing hair, but her face looked fuller and her ribs weren't showing anymore. She now had all the food she wanted, not how much she earned.

"Fuck you, Peters," she whispered to her reflection. "Fuck you all."

She turned away from the hatred flooding her eyes. *No time for hate, only time to live.*

The lukewarm water flowed over her as she poured the first bottle. She didn't need shampoo but she grabbed the bottle anyway and squeezed a handful of strawberry goodness into her hand. Rubbing it over her head and body was the best she'd felt in a long time.

She was pouring the second bottle over her head when the screams began again. Cursing, with shampoo in her eyes, she did the best she could and grabbed a towel to whip around her body.

"Emily. Emily. Emily. Emily."

"Shit, "Miranda said, as she ran into the bedroom.

Seth had pulled a hand free. She grabbed it as she jumped on the bed and straddled his hips. "Shush," she begged, putting her other hand over his mouth.

His movements slowed and stopped. He pulled his hand free and put it on the back of her neck. Pressure forced her to lean down over him. Her hand fell from his mouth seconds before he pulled her closer and his lips found hers. No forcing needed then. Oh my God, his kiss was heat and fire and sin. Everything she'd read about in romance novels and nothing like Peters' wet slurping on her face and in her mouth. Her head grew light and colors flashed behind her closed eyelids.

His lips left hers and trailed over her cheek to the sensitive skin behind her ear. His teeth nibbled at her earlobe and her legs grew weak. The only thing stopping her from collapsing on his body was the hand on her neck.

"Emily," he whispered in her ear.

She whimpered. Steel flashed up her spine. She removed his hand and put it on the covers. Slowly, she stopped straddling his hips and moved from the bed. Untying his other hand, she moved to his feet and untied them as well. Seth rolled to his side and settled into a comfortable sleep, snoring included. She covered him and backed out of the room.

"Damn, Emily, you are a lucky woman," she whispered, wiping a tear from her cheek.

Seth's eyes fluttered open. Pain shot from his hand, up his arm, to his head. He grabbed his hand and screamed in agony. Opening his eyes, his gaze traveled over his bandaged hand. The shape was wrong. He ripped the gauze off and it fell to the bed. He knew something was wrong, but his brain couldn't comprehend how this mutilated—burned thing could be his hand.

He sat up in the bed, the covers falling off. A whispered sound had his head spinning around. A young boy stood in the doorway. No. His view of the front of a T-shirt changed that thought. A young girl stood there. Flashes of her being there bombarded his mind.

A flash pierced his mind of the destroyed hospital.

Another flash slammed into him, of his mother turning into one of *them*.

His breath left him. His mother was dead. He'd killed his mother.

"Fuck."

"Yep, that about sums it up."

He winced. "Sorry about that."

She laughed. "No problem, Seth."

He sat up straighter. "How do you know me? Where are we? How did we get here? Are there others?"

"Whoa," she said, walking across the room and sitting on the bed beside him. "One thing at a time."

She gathered up the bloody gauze and rolled it into a ball. "Let's get that covered again."

When she left, he heard her in cabinets, presumably the bathroom. His hand throbbed where his missing fingers should be. It beat in time with his heart. He prayed there were some painkillers wherever she was.

"How do you know me?" It shot out the second she returned with gauze and 'Thank God' a pill bottle.

She cradled his hand, her fingers soft and sure. He looked away until she'd covered it up again. Shaking out a couple of pills into his other hand, she waited until he threw them in his mouth and handed him a water bottle.

"Sorry about that," she said, pointing to the bandages.

"Did you do that?"

"I had to. Let me start at the beginning. I'm Miranda Stevens. I saw you at Peters' compound in the Delta when you brought supplies and stuff."

His mouth dropped open. Miranda Stevens had been a beautiful young woman. She'd had brown hair to her waist and a smile for him every time he'd arrived with stuff for the group. He'd known some young man was going to be very lucky to win Miranda's heart someday. He couldn't reconcile that vivid memory of a sweet girl with the tough soldier chick before him.

She blushed, brushing a hand over her buzzed head. "It's not important. I don't want to discuss it."

"No problem," Seth added quickly, sorry he'd upset the young girl. "How did we get here? I remember the hospital." He swallowed harshly, his throat dry and tight.

"I found you after I escaped the General and his men. You had a woman in your arms. I figured she was your mom. She looked like you. So I buried her, the best I could, and got you here. Someone bit you. It didn't look so bad so I cut off your fingers, cauterized the wound, and waited for you to heal or turn. Whichever came first."

He stared at his hand. She talked so matter-of-factly of doing the things she'd done to save his life, but they couldn't have been easy. From the conversation, he got that there was only the two of them here. Wherever here was.

"How long since...since the hospital? What happened there?"

"It's been four days, no, maybe five, since General Peters and his zombie horde took the hospital."

"Took the hospital? Zombie horde?"

"He has a way to control them, to use them to attack people. He's going to The Streets of Brentwood next. He destroys everything he touches. God, I hate him."

"The Streets," Seth cried, jumping up. He collapsed back to the bed, the blood leaving his head. "I have to go. I have to warn them."

"Seth," Miranda said, placing a hand on his arm. "That was five days ago. Whatever was going to happen, has happened."

"But...Emily."

"You called for her in your sleep. A friend?"

He took her hand in his. "More than a friend."

"I'm sorry."

Seth dropped her hand. He put his palm over his eyes and hot tears scalded his face. *Emily couldn't be dead. She just couldn't be.*

His tears dried as fast as they had come. All this world did was take, take, take. Well, he was damned tired of it taking; it was time to take it back. It didn't belong to the undead bastards and it didn't belong to the General Peters of the world either.

He pushed himself off the bed with his good hand. "Where are my clothes?"

Miranda walked to a chair and brought him a pile with jeans and a shirt he didn't recognize. She shrugged. "Your shirt was too far gone, but I found a Goodwill store down the street and got you those. I figured you might like some clean jeans too."

He forgot and tried to grab the material with his right hand. A hiss escaped him as he jumped back when the denim brushed his injury. The pile fell between them. He cradled his hand as Miranda bent down and got the clothing for him.

His face heated. He was not going to be an invalid. What were a few fingers? At least, he was alive. He'd seen truckers in the past with missing parts of fingers. Just one of the many hazards of being a truck driver. He could do this.

Seth took the clothes from Miranda. "You shouldn't have done this. It's too dangerous to wander around by yourself for some jeans and T-shirts."

She blushed. "It wasn't so bad. I've seen hardly any undead at all. I think most of them died at the hospital."

She turned to go. "I'll let you get dressed. There's some fruit and veggies in the kitchen when you're ready."

He started to speak up, but the young woman had already gone out the door and shut it behind her. Dropping the stuff on the bed, Seth struggled to get out of his jeans and pulled on the new pair. He managed most of the way with minimal cursing and grabbing of his damaged hand. He zipped up the jeans but couldn't manage the button with one hand.

Letting it go, he slid a shirt over his head and called himself dressed. He paced the floor. Standing still just gave him time to mourn Emily, his mother, his old life. This world handed out nothing but crap. He'd told Emily that life mattered as long as they had it. She'd been right to see it for the load of bullshit it was. This wasn't life. This wasn't living. This was a big cosmic joke, and God was laughing at them all.

A sob built and broke loose as he slid to the floor, his head in his one good hand, the mangled one dangling by his side.

CHAPTER FIFTEEN

Highway 4
Between Concord and Brentwood

Martin Peters slammed his fist into the man's face.

Again.

And again.

And again.

Each crunch of bone eased his anger, until he released the man's shirt and turned away as he slid to the ground. He glared at the rest of the huddled group in lab coats, the women crying and the men staring at the ground.

"Damn it," he growled, striding into their midst. "I need a real doctor and I need it now."

Four days and four doctors and still no one could tell him if Tanya would live or die. He glanced over to the tent set up in the middle of the road, Antonio's crying carried on the silent air.

After the attack at the hospital, he'd returned to the bus to find Tanya twitching on the floor in the middle of a puddle of her own blood and his whore, Miranda, nowhere to be found. He'd dragged several men from their raping and pillaging to search. She hadn't been found.

He clenched his fists. When he found that little bitch he'd make her wish satisfying his sexual needs was all she had to do. When he got through with her, she'd be happy to hump the zombies to escape his twisted punishments.

The first doctor had refused to help him. Martin shot him in the head and pointed the gun at the next lab coat. The second doctor had been out of her element, but she'd tried. Martin gave her to the men after Tanya started convulsing.

The third doctor had been a general practitioner and might have helped Tanya if the woman hadn't hidden she'd been bitten and tried attacking her patient. Antonio had yanked her off Tanya and thrown her out of the tent for Martin to shoot. The fourth doctor lay bleeding at his feet, finally acknowledging that he was only an anesthesiologist and had no clue why Tanya wasn't waking up yet. Martin raised his hand and shot him in the head.

He kicked the dead man and strode over to the older woman in the group. "What kind of doctor are you?" he demanded, placing his gun barrel on her forehead.

She didn't blink. "The kind who knows that

woman is going to die if we don't release the bleeding on her brain. I can try to help her, but it might kill her too. What assurances do I have that you won't kill me if she dies?"

He squatted down in front of her, moving the gun to her chest. "None at all."

The woman glared into his face. "Well, I might as well try then."

Martin held out his other hand to help her up. She ignored it and pushed herself to her feet. He stepped aside. "This way, doctor…"

"Dr. Johnson, but you can call me Gwen." She marched up to the tent and pushed the flap back.

He followed her inside and grimaced at Antonio's wails. *It's my woman too, and you don't see me carrying on, do you?*

Gwen pulled a rubber band off her wrist and pulled back her long, auburn hair. She squatted by Tanya's cot and reached out to take her pulse. "It's fast and shallow. We need to get started right away. I can't believe I'm going to say this, but I need alcohol, scissors, and a drill."

Martin bellowed orders to his men and in short order the doctor had the things she needed. The blood left his face and his heart pounded when Gwen collected the scissors, a bottle of Jack Daniels, and a battery-powered drill like he'd had back home in his garage. His meal threatened to leave his stomach. He swallowed it back down. He was the leader, damn it.

"I don't need you here if you're going to throw up all over the place," the doctor snapped at him. "But I'm going to need someone to help hold her down."

Martin scanned the tent for Tanya's husband, but he was already kneeling in a corner with his rosary beads wrapped around his hands. *Fat lot of good that's going to do, Gomez. God helped those who helped themselves. If I do nothing else, I always help myself.*

"What else do you need, doctor?"

"Well, in a perfect world, a hospital and sterile conditions, I'd have clamps to keep her still and an anesthesiologist to knock her out, but you just killed the only one we had. Since we don't have any of that, we need to strap her down and immobilize her head. Without clamps, I'm thinking good, old, all-purpose Duct tape should do the job. But I'll still need you to hold the rest of her still."

His mouth dropped open and he stared at the petite woman in front of him.

"What, did you expect me to whine and cry when you'll probably kill me anyway? Sorry, buddy, but I stopped crying four months ago when I had to shoot my teenage daughter in the head. At least if I die today, I'll be able to see my Monica again."

His face heated in a rush with shame in a way it hadn't in more years than he cared to remember. Just as quickly, he stomped on it. He turned to the side and coughed. "If she lives, so do you."

She sighed. "I guess in this wonderful new world, that's all we can ask for."

He strode to the tent opening, demanded tape and got it. Martin returned to Tanya's cot and started taping her down. His fingers brushed against her cold, clammy skin. Only the slow up-and-down movement of her chest reassured him of her continued survival.

Kneeling by her side, he handed the tape to the doctor and waited as she ran it across Tanya's forehead and attached it to the cot. He jumped when Gwen grabbed a handful of his lover's dark, thick hair and the scissors. "Do you have to cut it all off?"

"I suppose at this point it doesn't really matter." She sectioned off a small area and cut the hair to the scalp in a three-inch square. She grabbed the bottle of Jack, poured some on the scalp and some on her hands. Picking up the drill, she coated the drill bit with more alcohol. She pressed the trigger to test the charge.

Martin jumped at the loud sound in the still, hot tent. He reached over and locked his hands onto Tanya's arms. "Ready."

"Okay," the doctor announced. "There is going to be some blood. I don't have all the tools I need here, so this is the best we've got."

"Just do it," he gritted out between his clenched jaws.

The drill whirred in the quiet. Blood spurted out of Tanya's scalp, but not as much as he was expecting, nothing like the puddle in the bus. He felt her bones creak beneath the tightened hands he'd clamped onto her arms. The sound of the drilling seemed to go on forever. The whine dug into his brain. He saw Tanya's eyeballs move beneath her eyelids, but she made no movement on the cot.

Finally, the noise stopped and the doctor dropped the drill to the tent floor and fell backward to her butt. She grabbed the bottle, poured some on her bloodstained hands, and then brought the bottle to her mouth. "Now, we wait," she muttered in between gulps.

"How long?" he whispered.

"Oh, I say the next twenty-four hours will tell." She handed the bottle to him. "No more of that. I'll keep watch with the husband there. He is the husband, right?"

She looked at him with a question in her tired eyes. A question he had no intention of answering. He stared until she turned away. "For now," he muttered under his breath as he stepped out of the tent.

◆◆◆

Darkness was everywhere. They were coming to get her; she could feel them holding her down, smothering her. Pressure in her head had her screaming but no sound came out. Nothing but darkness and silence. She tried to move, but they wouldn't let her. Her body was frozen and burning up at the same time.

"Martin, mi amor, where are you?" Tanya thought she spoke the words, but the words only echoed in her head.

"I'm right here, my love."

Tears filled her eyes and ran down her face and she wanted to scream. It wasn't the right voice. She hated that voice with a passion.

"Open your eyes," he pleaded. "Come back to me."

She fought to deny him, but her eyes opened anyway. She didn't see Antonio sitting in front of her. She didn't see anything at all. Darkness deeper than a moonless, starless night stared back at her. She screamed and nothing came out. No sound at all.

CHAPTER SIXTEEN

"Ten days. It's been ten whole days and nothing. Where in the hell is this zombie army?" I muttered to Michelle as we dug pit traps in front of the mall. It hadn't rained in months and the dirt was as hard as cement after the first few inches. Sweat covered my back and trickled down between my breasts to pool at my waistband. I missed the cool breezes off the bay. I even missed the fog.

My friend leaned on the shovel she held and wiped a forearm across her brow. "You should be happy they haven't shown up yet. Look at all we've accomplished." She swept her arm out to encompass what even in my irritated mood I had to acknowledge was amazing. We'd dug traps, rigged explosives to trip wires, and even in a worst-case scenario, rigged the mall to blow up with half of the supply of C-4 we had. If we were forced to fall back and leave it to the enemy, they sure as hell wouldn't have it for long.

"You're just so grumpy because you haven't

eaten enough lately," Michelle added as she continued to dig, the clunk of the shovel on the ground pounding in my head. "One meal a day doesn't cut it when we're out here digging ditches."

I fell to work, dizzy and nauseated again. "Dinner seems to be all I can keep down anymore. I visited the doctor like you said. I don't have the flu, Z or otherwise."

She shot a glance my way. Her eyes warmed with relief. I knew that look. We saw it every time someone coughed and went to see the doctor. The fear that the virus had mutated again and a person wouldn't have to die or get bitten to become a skinbag. Just another shitty problem to worry about among the ones we already had.

"I saw the scouts this morning when I was dry-heaving over the wall. Did they say anything to Jack?"

Michelle stopped digging and took off her neckerchief to wipe her face. "They went ten miles out and didn't find anyone. Commander Canida said he didn't want them going any further. They need to be able to beat the General and his crew back here if they spot them."

I put my hands on my waist and leaned backward, hearing and feeling the pops along my spine. I sighed in relief and got back to work. The sun beat down from overhead; we still had plenty of hours left to work. We couldn't waste any time of being prepared.

Hours later, as the sun finally started to set

in a fiery sky, we climbed out of our hole and helped the others put a tarp across the hole and scattered dirt, twigs, and leaves to cover it up. Not that the zombies would know the difference, but we might trap some of the humans as well. Bile rose in my throat, but I pushed it back down. We didn't start this fight. But we damned well would finish it. They should have left us the hell alone.

Every muscle in my body ached as I dragged myself to the showers set up in one of the old restaurants in the mall. We only had cold water, along with the last of the store-supply soap, but it washed the tiredness and grime away. Running my fingers through my hair, I could tell it was growing again as the wet ends touched my shoulders.

Pulling on clean jeans and a T-shirt, I headed to drop off my clothes at the laundry and find some food. My stomach grumbled audibly to let me know it had been too long since yesterday's dinner meal. I smiled. The thought of food didn't have me running to the nearest garbage can to toss my cookies, so that was good.

Spotting Michelle in the chow line, I rushed over and squeezed in beside her. "I'm starving."

"Of course you are. I told you earlier you can't work all day with no food. Even a Power Bar would have been something."

I shrugged. "Well, it doesn't do any good to eat breakfast if I'm just going to toss it off the rooftop. At least I'm fine by dinner."

I felt a bump behind me and turned to see Bobbie. "Maybe you should have Dr. Shannon give you another test."

"She already gave me a dozen tests. I'm not sick." I put my fingers up in the Girl Scout sign. "I swear."

"Maybe the doc should have given you a pregnancy test."

My mouth dropped open and stayed that way. Pain shot across my heart. "That is just cruel, Bobbie Roberts," I whispered, turning around.

"You know, my husband bred racehorses," Bobbie said to Michelle as I tried to tune her out. "Sometimes the mares just couldn't breed. Everyone thought it was the mare's fault, high-strung or whatever. Then they changed the stud. Before you knew it, the mare was pregnant."

Bobbie grabbed my shoulder and turned me to face her. She stared me straight in the eye. "Sometimes all you have to do is change the stud."

Another predawn heaving over the rooftop ledge and I went to Dr. Shannon for a pregnancy test. Heart racing a million miles an hour, I'd done the required pee and waited. Taking the test stick, I sat on the rooftop ledge by my tent and waited. I'd lost count of how many months I'd sat just like this—always waiting, always disappointed. Upset to see the anger in Carl's face. The unfair blame always placed firmly on me. The looks from his parents that screamed I was condemning the Gray lineage to extinction.

Did I want it to say positive or not? A stupid grin broke out on my face at the idea of a baby. All those wasted fertility treatments. All those hopeless months of thinking, 'maybe this time,' only to get my period—yet again. But just thinking of Nick and Beth reminded me yet again of why this was an impossible time to be pregnant. But wasn't any time an impossible time? If people waited for the 'right' time, there would be no babies at all.

A gasp escaped me as the test stick formed a plus sign in the little window, the sun rose behind me, and the bright rays illuminated shambling figures on the dirt fields and asphalt road as far as my eyes could see.

CHAPTER SEVENTEEN

"We're not an army," I said to Michelle, pointing. "Look at them. They have Jeeps, an armored school bus, and...and them." The blood left my head, leaving me light-headed and more scared than I'd been since the night of escaping San Francisco. A sea of rancid dead flesh waiting to turn us into more of the same took my breath away. Thoughts of suicide were too tempting.

They just stood there and swayed, their moans echoing off the buildings, sending shivers up my spine in spite of the heat. With the wind coming from the north, we were at least spared the reeking odor of the undead. That's all we were spared, as the 'general' marched back and forth in front of his Jeep, strutting about as if he owned the world. I conceded that with his zomb' army he could own what was left of the world we knew.

A tall, Hispanic man stood next to the Jeep with what looked like a synthesizer in front of him. According to the guy, Jed, he must be the one controlling the creatures. The cries of babies and children grated on my nerves along with the incessant hum that set my fillings to vibrating.

"Why can't they leave us alone? There's plenty for everyone. Wasn't the flu enough? Wasn't the rising of the dead enough? When does it stop?"

Michelle grabbed my arms and shook me. "I know it's the hormones talking. But shut up. If you aren't strong how am I supposed to be?" She'd taken the pregnancy test out of my hand and tucked it in my pocket. My mind was still blank. I hadn't had time to process whether it was good or bad news.

"Congratulations, by the way." She had the audacity to smile in the middle of all the chaos and certain death.

"How can you say congratulations? Are you insane?"

She handed me a rifle and my crossbow. "At least you have something to fight for now, don't you?"

My heart pounded in my chest, the beats thumping in my ears. I did have something to fight for, something so precious it took my breath away. I had someone other than just myself to worry about now. I looked around the rooftop at the tents and people. We'd created something great here and they couldn't have it. We'd destroy it ourselves before we let them have it.

The hum built to a crescendo in my head. I gritted my teeth and whipped my head around. Like so much cannon fodder they marched forward, their dead feet stumbling in the dirt of the field. Dust clouds billowed as the horde moved, their numbers hidden, but their rising moans hinting at hundreds.

Canida's bellow echoed up and down the rooftop. "Don't waste ammo. Let the traps do their work first. Only shoot if they get close to the walls."

They fell into the pits in large groups. A cheer went up on the rooftop. I stared as the general raised a gun to the Hispanic man. He pointed to the synthesizer repeatedly. The short man turned in a circle until he spotted another man and shot him through the heart.

I gulped hot dusty air. He had to know that the dead didn't stay dead. Proof was given as the shot man stood and started marching with the others. I raised my gun and sighted down the scope. The smirk on his face twitched on my last nerve. My finger touched the trigger. Shaking, I pulled it away. I'd never make the shot, it would just be a waste of a bullet, and staring at the horde, I knew we'd need every one. Our ammo was limited, the zombies weren't.

Explosions went off and filled the air with blood, guts, and dirt. The Claymore mines we'd placed as the next line of defense were doing their job, destroying the suicide bombers before they could destroy our walls. I'd laughed at the time at the stupid easy directions of *Front toward Enemy*. Seeing the carnage steel balls could cause wasn't so laughable now, even if the enemy was undead. I dry heaved on nothing but bile.

The stench of the zombies reached us as the undead reached the walls. Firing straight down made it easier to hit the head but the bodies started piling up and the skinbags just climbed over the pile like army ants trying to get to the fresh meat they must smell now that they were so damned close. Their moans ratcheted up as the pile grew and they inched closer.

Running up and down the wall, I tried to spread out the kills. The men near me followed suit and dead bodies formed smaller and smaller piles. An explosion rocked the building as the zombie's vests were detonated. Flesh and dirt flew into the air. Dust blocked my breathing and my vision. Screams filled the air. I'd never understood the insanity of going to war and I didn't understand it now. Even saving humanity didn't seem worth this—this abomination.

Staring down at the wall, I saw blackened bricks. Further down the building, near the biggest pile, a giant hole gaped through the bricks. The undead spilled into the opening with live men following right behind. My heart stopped beating. Canida rushed to our side of the building.

"Emily, hold this side with the Alpha group. Beta will fall back to the ground and take out the ones who make it inside."

I grabbed a few men and women and pointed to the field beyond. "Shoot anything that moves on two legs. Even a leg shot will slow them down."

Turning, my gaze followed Canida and his group as they sprinted down the wooden stairs. I whipped my head back around as guns started firing into the mass below. My bladder wanted to let go as my flight mentality tried to kick in.

Metallic booms rang out as the zombies reached the steel cargo containers blocking the streets into the shopping center. I grabbed Michelle's shoulders and screamed into her ear. "That's it. Round up the women, children, and babies and get out of here. I'll meet you at the retreat site."

"I'm not leaving without you," she cried out. "You have to come too." Her hands dug into my arm.

"I'll be right behind you. I'm not a martyr." I touched my stomach. "I'll be there. I promise."

Waiting until she gathered the women on the roof, I turned back to the front. The echo of the stampede down the stairs wafted over me as I sighted and shot with the rifle until it clicked empty. Throwing it down, I grabbed my crossbow over my shoulder and shot until my bolts were gone. Tossing it back, I turned to leave with the rest of the group. A light flashed off something in the field. I yanked up a gun and sighted with the scope. There it was again. A glint of something shone on one of the skinbags. At one time he had been a man. His jeans and blue T-shirt were encrusted with blood and gore. Green glimmered in his ear. The rifle dropped from my tingling hands. I pulled the forgotten binoculars to my eyes and zoomed in. A shamrock earring glimmered in its ear.

"Seth!" My cry carried across the field.

It was him. It wasn't him. My mind splintered. I had to know. How could I leave without knowing for sure? Temporary silence filled the rooftop. Everyone but me was gone. Running to the rope ladder, I threw it down over the side of the building. I grabbed a handgun and checked it for bullets. One left. All I would need.

My feet slipped as I rushed down the rope. I fell the last few rungs and stumbled to the ground. Only the ragged sound of my breathing filled my ears. The battle's din was lost to the thumping heartbeat in my ears. I weaved and dodged the skinbags left in the field. Stumbling, I almost fell into a pit, jumping around the edge of it instead, dirt crumbling under my feet and undead hands reaching for me.

I skidded to a stop in front of the thing that had been a man. The hum had him intent on reaching the walls. His gaze skittered over me as if I wasn't there.

The hair left on his head was the right color. The eyes behind the opaque shield were light enough to be hazel. The earring was Seth's, I knew it. My fingers clawed at the suicide vest and ripped it off his chest. I threw it behind me. His shirt was in tatters, along with the flesh below. If he'd had a tattoo there, I'd never know now. I screamed his name, hoping against all logic that he'd notice me; as if some remnant of my lover still existed in this bag of flesh and bones before me.

A massive explosion rocked the world and tore the silence to shreds. Ringing filled my ears. I stumbled with my equilibrium thrown off. Dust and debris filled the air, along with blood and gore. I turned and the shopping center was a pile of rubble. Bricks and body parts rained down across the dusty field. Something flew in the air toward me. I flung my hands up, but it hit my head. Pain, and then nothing as black emptiness filled my vision.

◆ ◆ ◆

"Who is that warrior goddess?" Martin Peters said, watching the dark-haired woman shimmy down the rope ladder and run across the field of zombies. She'd screamed something and taken off like a shot toward a shambling undead. He held his breath as she'd ripped off the vest full of explosives and flung it away.

A crack of sound filled the sky as the shopping center buildings imploded, flames shooting into the air, and the wave of superhot air throwing debris and dust into their midst. He turned and covered his face. Even with a thousand bombers he couldn't have caused the explosion.

"Damn them," he yelled. Canida and his people had to have caused it. As the dust cleared, he had a straight view to what was left of the fortress. Piles of rubble replaced the buildings that would have housed him and his men this winter. A few undead shuffled around the debris, but most were buried under mounds of bricks and mortar. His men were the only live people he saw. He picked up a rock and threw it across the field.

"Fall in," he bellowed, counting as his men ran to the vehicle from their locations around the open space. "Ten," he whispered, the blood leaving his head. *Twelve if you counted him and Antonio. A few worthless doctors and Tanya still unconscious in the bus.*

He straightened his spine and stood tall. "Gather all the weapons you can find. Head shots to anyone you see, alive or undead. Then we'll check out the shopping center. They couldn't have gotten everything out. Fall out. We leave in one hour."

Antonio's fingers moved over the keyboard and the undead scattered as far away as they could get. "We're going to need fuel for the generator if you find it. We need this running more than weapons."

"Understood," Martin muttered under his breath. If he only knew how the man did it, Antonio would be gone.

Peters walked across the field toward where he'd seen the dark-haired woman. Sporadic shots rang out as his men zigzagged across the field. He stopped every few feet to grab a weapon or shoot the undead still crawling along the ground, trying to escape the humming sound.

He dropped the guns in his arms as he approached the woman. She lay unmoving on the ground. A crossbow was strapped over her shoulder. He smiled. What a beautiful weapon. He wanted it. Nudging her with his foot, she lay there dead. He shrugged. A pity. What a waste. She had been even more beautiful than Tanya. And brave. A warrior. He would have liked to beat her into submission. Had her begging for a mercy he didn't have.

He reached for the crossbow and pulled, but it wouldn't come. He grabbed a shoulder and rolled her over. A bruise was forming on her temple and blood leaked across her face. Finding a buckle on the strap for the crossbow, he squatted down and his fingers worked the buckle. A moan startled him. Her eyelids lifted and dark, deep eyes stared at him with intelligence.

"What in the fuck are you doing?"

He grinned, raised his fist, and struck her on the bruised temple. She slipped back into unconsciousness with a small whimper. He gathered her up and flung her limp body over his shoulder. He walked right past the pile of guns. Let his men get them. He'd found something better than any weapon; he had an insurance policy if Tanya didn't wake up.

.

CHAPTER EIGHTEEN

To die. To sleep. Ripped from us.
To die. To Hell. Taken from us.
Hell is to live.
Heaven is a wisp, a vapor, a lie.
— Seth Ripley

Had it been two weeks, or three? Seth shook his head. He didn't know anymore. The days blended one into another in a heated-oven feel of Indian summer. The calendar said October, the weather said mid-July. He grabbed the bandana off his neck and scrubbed the sweat from his face, before tucking it into his back pocket. Yearning for the bay breeze he missed, he pushed up his shirt sleeves and hacked at another zombie with his machete. He wiped the blood on its shirt and moved to the next, kicking the finally dead thing to the side.

Clearing the area each day sapped his energy, but it assured they got a peaceful rest at night. The sound of the girl fighting at his back had become reassuring in a short time.

"I feel like a packrat," she said between loud whacks of her own machete. "All we do is fight, gather food, and sleep."

"This sucks," they intoned together, and then laughed.

"Beats the alternative," he grunted back, pulling the steel from a skull with a sickening sound.

He kicked the body to the side. "I've got two more."

"I've got one," Miranda added.

Whack.

"I'm done."

"Me, too," Seth added. He wiped the blade clean and scanned the area. Calming his breathing, he sighed as silence filled the street. No moans. No shuffling of dead feet. *The dead are now dead. About fucking time.*

He pulled the bandana out of his pocket and wrapped it around his face, covering his nose and mouth. The small market had intact glass windows, promising the possibility of canned goods. Also, promising the reek of decomposed fruits, vegetables, and meat.

They stepped through the door with a jangle of a bell. Seth tensed and waited, Miranda silent at his back. Nothing. He breathed in and regretted it instantly as the miasma of months-old food filled the tiny bodega.

Seth headed to the tiny aisle of canned soups and vegetables. Miranda passed on his right, headed for the soap and deodorant section. The undead might track them better when they smelled fresh, but he wasn't ready to give up all comforts yet. Someday there would be no more soap unless someone out there knew the old way of making it. Until then he would enjoy it.

"We should find a library," he whispered in the darkened store. "Find some of those how-to books. Maybe a doomsday prepper wrote some."

Miranda giggled in the back of the store. "Who knew those guys had it right all along?"

Seth sobered up quickly. They had had it right. Why had everyone, himself included, laughed at them? If it hadn't been the Z flu, it would have been something else. Something always came along to cull the herd when it got too big. Always.

"I think I saw a library the other day. Two

streets over. To the west." Miranda's voice pulled him back from his dismal thoughts.

"Let's get this stuff back to the apartment. Maybe we'll see the building from one of the windows."

Miranda strode to his side with a bulging burlap sack. He hefted his full knapsack to his back and they headed out, this time with his hand holding the bell from jangling. A quick scan of the street showed a few shamblers at least three blocks away. Nothing to worry about.

A swift run down the block and they were back to the apartment building they called home for the moment.

◆ ◆ ◆

Miranda ran a hand over her buzzed head. Without taking his eyes from the binoculars, he jerked her hand down. "Leave it alone, it's growing," he grunted.

"Fine," she mumbled.

"I can see a book deposit box on the corner on the next block. The library must be the one with the red tile roof."

Seth handed her the binoculars. She put them up to her eyes and stared in the direction he pointed. "Yep, says Public Library on it. Do you think it will be crowded? Would people have gone there in an emergency?"

"Not sure," he said as he grabbed his rifle and pulled the strap over his shoulder. "Probably not. Most evacuation centers in a disaster are large, open buildings. Gyms and armories."

She handed the binoculars back to Seth. His injured hand reached for them and missed, the strap finding nothing to catch on with his missing fingers. A muttered oath slipped out as he kicked them across the room.

"I'm sorry," she whispered.

He reached over and pulled her close. "You don't have to be sorry. You saved my life, Ran."

She smiled at his new nickname for her. Her heart beat wildly as she gazed up at his hard, handsome face. Her hands reached and grabbed his face. Before she could think, she pulled his face to hers and kissed him. His lips were warm and soft and tender against hers. For a perfect second, he kissed her back.

With a groan, he pulled away. "Don't do that. You're a child."

"General Peters didn't think I was a child." She knew she was hurt and pouting like a child, but she didn't care. She had been there for Seth and he had been there for her. They belonged together. "I'm nineteen and a half."

He pushed her against the wall until her spine hit. Not hard, but not soft either.

"If you have to add 'and a half' that just shows how young you are. Don't ever compare me to that monster. He took everything. Your innocence. Your father. My mother. Emily."

The last name left his lips on a shaking stutter she felt through her body. "You don't know she's dead. Not really."

"I saw what they did to the hospital. No way did the Streets group survive that. They're all gone and I'm sure Peters is lording it over Brentwood from the compound. No one is going to stop him. With his zombie army, he'll take over the whole area. Hell, the whole state."

"We could go see," she whispered, staring at the floor. Part of her really wanted them to go so Seth could see everyone was dead and he could move on. Another part of her wanted the Streets group to have won and to know for sure that Martin Peters was dead and gone.

Seth stepped back and crossed his arms on his chest. "There is a saying about revenge, about digging two graves."

She'd heard that saying in English class. It didn't matter. "So he just gets away with what he's done? To everyone. To me."

He didn't say a word. Just gathered his weapons and headed to the door. She followed, her head held high.

I'm willing to die, if it means I take Peters with me.

An intense ten minutes later, and they reached the library with limited killing. Seth used a machete and she used a small pick-axe she'd picked up at a hardware store. The door to the building stood open, with darkness as far as she could see inside.

Turning, she checked out the street as Seth

made his way through the entrance with her following. She held her breath as he snapped a Glo stick and rolled it across the floor. It came to rest against a pile of papers. Her heartbeat sped up at the comforting, familiar smell of books and the graham crackers of story time. *Don't let there be kids.*

An exhaled breath left her as silence filled the building. No moans, no shambling footsteps, no voices telling them to put their hands up. She took a chance. Although it seemed wrong for a library, she breathed in and called, "hello" in a loud voice.

"Well, you couldn't have come for food, since there isn't any. And I'm pretty sure there isn't anyone left to help you check out a book anymore."

Her breath caught in her throat. A young man walked toward them, his hands in the air. He looked to be about her age, but the calm tranquility on his face made him appear much younger. With the bleached blonde, spiky hair and his cargo shorts, his whole persona screamed surfer dude.

"Hi, I'm Cody Taylor. You're the first real people I've seen in weeks."

Seth held his hand up for silence. Moans echoed from the street. He strode over and slowly shut and locked the door. As he walked back over, she stared at Cody. The man looked like he was just hanging out in the ZA until the next killer wave hit.

Seth came over with outstretched arms and herded them toward the back of the library. "Where have you been staying?" he asked while they walked down the aisle.

The young man pointed to a staircase in the corner. "There's a loft upstairs."

Seth waved the kid ahead and they followed.

◆ ◆ ◆

He smiled as Miranda squealed like the young girl she still was in so many ways once she spied Cody Taylor's collection of weapons nailed and hung on far wall. Seth's smile broadened as well at the sight of several AR-15's and even a rocket launcher.

A few candles provided enough light to see all the corners of the loft. The area was spacious but not over large. He moved to where the kids stood as Miranda asked about the weapons.

"The armory is about a mile or so away on the west side of town. I hit there the first week. The soldiers were undead or gone. I had my car back then, but it's too dangerous to drive around now unless you have a tank. The remnants follow you like a herd of cows at sunset."

"Remnants?" she asked.

"That's what I've been calling them. They're just the remnants of who they were. Like, when we die and our soul leaves. Our bodies are just shells."

"Where's the rest of your group?" Seth butted in, the subject too close to how his mother used to talk for comfort.

"No group. I've been alone since it happened. Came home from Sac State as fast as I could." His gaze shot around the library. "My mom was librarian here."

Seth stared in amazement as Miranda sat down on the couch and patted the seat next to her for the boy. "You didn't find her?"

"Ran," he said, glaring at her.

"What? Like it isn't the first question everyone asks. Where were you? How did you get here? Where is your family?"

Cody's face brightened a little. "Like I said, I was at Sac State. Junior year. Majoring in economics." He laughed. "Great choice, right? I should have joined Future Farmers of America or something. I drove here. The freeway most of the way, over the hills and through fields the rest of the time. Mom was it. All I had."

Miranda grabbed his hand. "You didn't find her, did you?" she asked again in a whisper that Seth just caught.

"No, I thought she would be here since she wasn't at the house." He swallowed with an audible click. "And I haven't seen her outside...yet."

"And you guys?"

Seth winced at the question. He still had nightmares from the hospital. He rubbed where his fingers should be. Constant rubbing seemed to be toughening the area up. Every day they were a little less sensitive to touch.

Miranda thankfully piped up first. "I lived out in Knightsen."

At his puzzled look, she added, "In the boonies, out on the Delta."

"Did you live there with your family? You know, after."

She squared her shoulders and Seth took a step forward but Cody seemed to be doing okay with the girl. The young man grabbed both her hands. "I'm sorry."

"No problem," she said with the fakest smile Seth had ever seen on her. "We lived in a compound for a while until the leader came here to Concord to attack the hospital a few weeks ago."

"I think I remember that," Cody said. "I heard a bunch of vehicles and I was going to run outside but the moans of the remnants filled the streets. I couldn't figure out why I didn't hear a bunch of shooting and yelling. The whole town was quiet except for 'them.'"

"They were leading the zombies. They made them into an army."

"No fucking way," he added, and then turned to Seth. "What about your family, dude?"

"My mother was at the hospital," he intoned and turned away, rubbing where his fingers should be. He pulled his hand away when he saw he was doing it again. Time to forget and move on.

"So, um. Tell me about this zomb army thing," Cody piped up too loud.

Seth turned away as Miranda explained the impossible. His mind traveled to Brentwood and Emily. He wanted to pray it had been fast, but praying wasn't something he turned to anymore. The man upstairs wasn't at home. And his mother wasn't here to remind him.

Because, he'd killed her.

Okay, maybe the zombies killed her, but he'd finished the job.

CHAPTER NINETEEN

Blood dripped from my wrists as I pulled at the handcuffs for what seemed the millionth time. It felt like the metal was rubbing on my bones. But it was just another pain to add to the list. I stared at my stomach and whispered a thank-you to God there was no pain there. The baby inside me might only be a collection of cells so far, but it contained Seth and I hoped that meant God was watching over him or her.

"That will be all, Captain Gomez," a voice intoned outside the room. My skin crawled as the man who called himself General entered the room and shut the door behind him without a sound.

He paced back and forth in front of my outstretched feet. "I hate to keep calling you woman. It sounds so impersonal. And bitch sounds rude for love-making."

I shuddered at his lewd words and my limbs shook as adrenaline flooded my system. It took all I had to keep my voice calm and low. "What you are thinking of doing wouldn't be love-making. Don't try to convince yourself that you'd be doing anything other than raping me."

Faster than I expected, he straddled my hips and gripped my face in his hands. "I have not raped you...yet."

His hand slipped from my face and grabbed my breast hard. Nothing would be better than vomiting on him right then, but for the first time this week my stomach wasn't cooperating. His other hand seized my hair and pulled my head back. His wet lips traveled down my neck and my stomach roiled. His fingers tangled in my necklace and he pulled. It scratched my neck as he ripped it off and flung it away.

"You are a hot bitch. But I bet you know that. Were you Canida's? That bastard thought he could have it all—the fortress, the weapons, the women."

It hurt to think of Canida and the rest of the people of The Streets. I didn't know how many had survived. I'd only seen the dead when General Peters dragged us through the rubble that was all that was left of the so-called fortress. We'd stumbled upon my friend, Bobbie, her body destroyed by the blast she'd caused, the detonator grasped in her dead hand.

A whimper broke from my throat and a shudder ran down my shaking body. Peters must have thought it was passion because he twisted my breast until I thought he meant to tear it off. He ground his pelvis to mine and I wanted to die.

"Why don't you go fuck your whore?"

He jumped up like a cattle prod zapped his groin. "What did you say?"

I stared him straight in the eye. "I've heard the men talking about your slut. She's in a coma. Guess that makes it easier for you."

A flash of flesh tone was all I saw before his backhand connected with my cheek. Lights exploded in my head. I opened my eyes to see his leg pulled back to kick me. Tucking myself into a tight ball, I prayed that I could protect the life inside me.

"General Peters," a voice called out as the one I thought was Captain Gomez opened the door and stepped inside. "An old man is at the perimeter who wants to barter some food and some women."

"Well," he said, waving the other man out the door. "Let's see what he has that we can steal."

He turned to me and sank his fingers into my chin. "I'll be back tonight and you'll find out what it means to be my whore."

He stepped back and I tried to kick him, but he just moved out of my reach and laughed at my attempts. His cackles echoed as he shut the door and I heard the lock turn.

Yanking on the handcuffs, I chastised myself. "Stupid. Stupid. Stupid. You should have sweet talked him, Emily. It might have gotten the handcuffs off. Then you could have escaped, you idiot."

My bitter, harsh laugh startled me. How far I'd come from a pampered San Francisco society wife to even consider giving myself to some sadistic asshole to get away. I shook my head. What a world. Rape or zombies. Not a great choice, but I'd still take my chances with the undead over Peters.

My eyelids started drooping as the sun left the gap high on the broken wall. From the early-morning tension of taking the pregnancy test, to the exhaustion of the battle, to the terror of my capture, this had been the longest day of my life. Even my grumbling stomach demanding food wasn't enough to keep me awake. I slept off and on as my weight pulled on my arms and the handcuffs ripped at my wrists. Blood trickled down my arms. Connected to the wall, they'd become dead weight hours ago, all the feeling drained away in my current position.

A key turned in the lock and I awoke in an instant. I kept my eyelids closed as the door opened and quietly shut again. A citrus scent tickled my nose and I cracked an eyelid enough to see a man standing in front of me with a small lantern. He was too tall to be the Napoleon Complex-infected Martin Peters. Squatting in front of my legs, the man whispered, "Are you awake?"

Whatever he wanted, it wasn't as if I could fight him. Opening my eyes, I saw the Hispanic man; the one Peters called Captain Gomez. He put a finger to his lips and held up a small silver handcuff key as he sat the lantern on the floor.

The surprise must have shown on my face because he smiled. He reached and a couple of clicks announced my arms were free. I pulled them down and he grabbed the cuffs and tossed them on the bed.

"Here, sit on the cot," he whispered as he pulled me up and I fell to the hard surface. "Your arms have been up there for a while, so it is really going to hurt when they come back to life. Please be quiet or we both die. I meant to get you out earlier with the doctors, but I had to wait for the guards to be occupied."

Biting my lip, I groaned as quiet as possible when the feeling did come back. A million paper cuts on the surface of my arms. Each only so painful, but unbearable when put all together. Tears slid down my cheeks.

He reached into his pocket and pulled out a medicine tube I assumed was ointment and some gauze bandages. "This may sting a little," he spoke softly as he rubbed the ointment on my wrists and bound them with the bandages, his touch as gentle as a mother's. "Fresh blood will attract the undead."

"Here, you haven't eaten all day," he said, pulling a squished and torn orange out of his pocket.

I yanked it out of his hand and bit into the skin to peel it, my fingers useless for the task at the moment. The scent of the orange filled my nostrils as I ate, peel and all. All too soon I was left with nothing but sticky fingers and a hunger that hadn't been satisfied.

"Okay, here is what you're going to do. The men are occupied with the putas on the east side of this place. The side where I think it was a soccer field at one time."

I pictured The Streets of Brentwood before it was destroyed. "Okay."

"The front is gone, between the zombies and your friends," he continued. "If you go out on the west side by the highway you should only have the undead to contend with."

He reached into his other pocket and pulled out a voice recorder. "This will help you. I put the repel sound on there, but I could only find a few batteries, so use it sparingly." His fingers were warm as he placed the recorder into my hands.

"Why didn't you put all of the sounds? When I find my friends, we could use them."

His brow furrowed and his eyes narrowed. "No one should have that kind of power. It should be enough that you will be able to keep them away. Control is too dangerous."

I couldn't say I didn't agree, with that saying about absolute power and corruption and all. I reached for his hand. "Are you coming with me? I'm sure the group would let you in."

He pulled away. "I'll get you to the edge of the mall. But I have things to do here. The time for vengeance is now."

A chill ran over my skin at his words. Darkness filled his gaze. Someone was going to die tonight.

"Captain Gomez," I started.

"Don't use that false name," he said. "I'm just Antonio."

"Antonio," I said, taking his hand again. "Leave this place. Leave these people. Forget Peters and his men and his whore."

He raised his hand and I flinched as it neared. It stopped inches from my face, his hand shaking before he pulled back.

"That is my wife you are talking about."

My mouth dropped open, and then I shut it with a snap. Okay. This was all so not my problem and all I wanted was to be gone. Some of the group must have escaped. There hadn't been enough dead to be everyone.

"I'll wait outside the door while you change and then I'll take you to the perimeter."

As he exited the room, I spotted the camo clothing he'd placed on the cot. Rushing to change, I threw my dirty, blood-splattered stuff to a far corner. The shirt was a little big, but a few rolls of the sleeves and I was good to go. I searched the dirt floor for my necklace, but not even a glimmer of silver showed. I stood up with a sigh. My last connection to my past life was gone.

Getting out of the collapsed building and to the edge of the mall was much easier than I had imagined. The men's yells of excitement barely echoed from the far end of the shopping mall. We reached the wall where just a short time ago I'd climbed down the rope ladder each day to go on patrol. Out of the corner of my eye, I spotted it blowing in the breeze.

Antonio reached and shook my hand. "Be safe, mujer guerrera."

"What does that mean?" I asked as I grabbed him in a hug.

He kissed my forehead and handed my crossbow to me. I snatched it like a long-lost friend.

"It means warrior woman," he replied, stepping back.

I slung the crossbow onto my back and grasped the recorder. "My name is Emily," I whispered.

"Good-bye, Emily."

I put my hand on my stomach. "Antonio, living well is revenge."

He stepped back into the shadows. "But dying well is sweeter."

I wanted to call out to him, but already I could hear the moans of the skinbags nearby and the catcalls of the men in the distance and his shadowy form was gone. Heading to the bypass road, I pictured the directions I'd memorized of location one and location two if we had to evacuate.

◆ ◆ ◆

The echo of moans and shambling feet trickled through to Martin's subconscious. He tossed and turned in his sleep and struggled to awake. He'd drunk too much before falling into bed beside Tanya. At least she didn't glare at him and belittle him like the dark-haired slut.

A whisper intruded. A shuffling of feet echoed. Adrenaline flooded his system and his eyes snapped open wide. Breath rushed from his nose and his mouth remained shut. Skin pulled as he tried to rip open his lips.

His mouth was taped shut. Probably from the large roll in Antonio's hands. The same hands tightened on the silver tape causing the knuckles to whiten under his deeply tanned fingers. His gaze traveled up to his captain's face. Anger and hatred narrowed the eyes and flattened the lips tightly. A look the man hadn't been brave enough or stupid enough to show before now.

I should have killed him.

He swallowed the bile rising in his throat. Vomiting would only hasten his death. A death he saw foretold in the man's cold, dark eyes. Turning his head, he stared at his lover. His breath caught as her chest slowly rose and fell. He closed his eyes and breathed as deep as possible. The man hadn't killed his cheating wife—yet.

A shadow fell across the bed and he opened his eyes again. Antonio stood over him. Pulling with his arms and legs, he struggled to rise from the mattress. His ankles were taped together and a rope stretched from his feet to across the room. A glance above his head showed a similar rope held his taped hands to a pipe in the wall.

The sound of a knife being pulled from a sheath yanked his attention back to the betrayed husband at his side.

Antonio squatted by the mattress and used

the knife to rip open Martin's shirt, exposing his soft flesh to the blade of a sharp knife. Ignoring his muffled screams, the man sliced across his chest and belly. The cuts deep enough to be agony, but not deep enough to kill. The stench of warm blood filled the room and wetness pooled under his back.

"Why now?" he screamed in his head. He'd been sleeping with Tanya for months. Hell, even before the influenza outbreak. Why wait 'til now to strike?

Antonio moved to the foot of the bed and pointed the bloodstained knife at him. The man's soft tones barely reached his ears.

"You had it all. A safe haven, weapons, food, and men to follow you. But that wasn't enough. You had to have this place." Antonio turned his hand toward the darkness.

Moans echoed off the fallen walls, increasing in loudness. Martin's heart raced. The now-familiar hum was gone. His gaze traveled to the corner where Antonio had set up the synthesizer and speakers. His heart stuttered to a dead stop at the sight of a pile of rubble. The equipment was destroyed, sitting there in pieces. Useless.

His captain's attention returned to him. "You had everything we needed to survive, but that wasn't enough."

His gaze followed as Antonio walked to the other side of the bed. Tanya's side. The woman was a princess in a deep sleep. Her dark hair cascaded over the side of the mattress, her dark, warm eyes hidden from him in her coma.

Antonio leaned over the woman. His hand brushed hair from her face, and then the same hand covered her mouth and nose. He pressed harder. Tanya moaned and moved slightly.

Martin struggled against his bound hands. His muffled yells couldn't penetrate the duct tape on his face.

Antonio glared at him, his hand never moving from his wife's face. "You could have any woman you wanted. There were plenty of women, women willing to use their bodies for protection. But you wanted my wife. Mine."

Tanya's struggles had ceased. No movement of her chest remained. Antonio moved back to the far wall, his face in the shadows. "Now I give her to you. You can be together forever."

Sweat poured off Martin's body as Tanya's limbs twitched and moans rose from her throat. Her eyes opened and a milky opaqueness filled them. Her jaw opened and closed and she sat up. Turning to her lover, the scent of fresh blood drove her on.

He screamed as she reached him.

He screamed as she fed on him.

He screamed as Antonio raised his hand, put the gun to his own head, and pulled the trigger.

He was still screaming as the other man's body hit the ground.

Jill James

CHAPTER TWENTY

The Lord is my Shepherd...
— Psalms 23:1-6 King James Bible

I was alone.

For the first time since all this crap started, I was alone.

Not on a bus full of other frightened people.

Not on a rooftop with friends and companions to this disaster.

Not on patrol with a partner. Not with Nick. My mind flashed to his young girlfriend, Beth and the baby she carried.

Not with Seth.

My hand moved to my stomach. A reminder at once beautiful and dangerous, that I'd never be alone again. Staying alive was no longer just about me. Breath caught in my throat. A part of that gentle man lived on. I pressed gently. Tears welled up in my eyes. Swiping hard at the wetness, I moved across the dirt field.

A spate of gunfire echoed from behind me and died away. The moans of the undead became fewer and far between as I cradled the recorder as gently as I would one day carry my baby. Dropping it was not an option. My aching fillings were a small piece to pay to walk in the dark untouched. Skinbags stumbled toward me, only to flee the other way as fast as their deteriorating legs and feet could carry them once they heard the hum.

My mind scrambled for a place to wait until sunrise. Having the recorder was all fine and dandy, but the batteries wouldn't last forever. If I could just find a place to rest without needing the sound, I could travel by daylight and only use it as needed.

The stench of the finally dead filled my lungs as I crouched and searched among the bodies for any weapons. The familiar weight of my crossbow might have filled me with more confidence if I'd had the bolts to go with it, but I'd used them all in the battle and I couldn't see where they'd pierced bodies in the dark.

The Moon peeked out from behind some clouds and gilded the strewn dead with a silver-edged dignity they'd certainly not had as walking skinbags. I whispered a small prayer and scrambled to find a couple of guns and a knife hopefully before the moonlight disappeared. A torn duffel bag yielded the mother lode—five handguns, a machete, and three knives, along with a heavy-duty flashlight. In daylight I could make my way to the Target group and trade for some supplies and bolts for the crossbow from their sports store—provided the sicko general hadn't hit them before us.

Silence filled the battlefield. A single gunshot rang out from the mall and then silence once more. No moans. No yells. No cries. No one was a winner in a zombie war.

Only the hum below the threshold of hearing from the recorder vibrated my eardrums. I slung the duffel bag on my shoulder and strode to the blacktop road. I stood in the intersection, the breeze sweeping from the north filling my lungs with untainted air. A choice had to be made.

I could go north toward Antioch and the Target group. I shook my head. Not in the dark. The general could have sent out patrols. They could be in command of the other shopping mall as well. Anything in that direction was too risky at night.

I could go south down the bypass, like on patrol. Just as iffy in the dark and empty of people—live people.

I could go west toward Mount Diablo. I'd never been that way and I didn't like the idea of finding out what was in that direction in the dark.

What about east? Not an option to go back past The Streets of Brentwood with possible guards at the other end, even though I couldn't hear them anymore.

An image flickered through my mind. A feature Nick had pointed out on that first patrol trip many months ago. Slightly southwest from the intersection was a water tank on the hillside. I'd asked what the grass-covered thing was and Nick had told me the water tank was covered with plants to hide it from the suburbanites by blending into the vegetation. Buy an expensive house and you didn't have to see anything as utilitarian as a water tank.

The Moon came out from behind the clouds and lighted my way under the unfinished overpass and across the rising field to the water tank. The smell of burned grass still clung to the field.

I reached the towering water tank. No blood or guts decorated the steel stair treads. I sniffed. No stench of the undead. Listening, only the hum of the recorder throbbed in my jawbone.

With a press of the button, I turned it off and

heard... nothing. One step at a time, I climbed to the top. An empty metal expanse greeted me. Moving to the center, I set down my crossbow and the duffel bag. The small thump echoed with a metallic ring.

Sitting with crossed legs, I faced the stairs and relaxed, taking my first deep breath in hours. My hands wandered over my still flatter than flat stomach. No cramps. No twinges.

Over the years, I'd become an unwilling expert in watching for the first signs of losing a baby. Thinking back over all the attempts, all the costs of treatments, and a few times with Seth and I was going to have a baby.

My thoughts didn't turn to Carl very often these days, but they did then. Would he have been different if I'd conceived? Sometimes, it was hard to dig up memories of the before.

Before the in vitro treatments.

Before the accusations started.

Before the infidelity began.

Mostly, it hurt too much to think of his anger at my 'fault,' when it hadn't been my fault at all.

A laugh escaped and turned into tears at the memory of Bobbi's comment of changing the stud. I scrubbed away the wetness. Seth had been so much more than a stud, a one-night stand. I could have loved him. I did love him. Him and the gift he'd left me. I wished he could know what he'd given me.

So many years had passed since I'd been thankful for anything, that it felt unfamiliar as I got to my knees, clasped my hands together, and looked to the sky and the stars above. Haltingly, the words came back.

"Dear Lord, in Jesus' name I pray. Thank you for bringing Seth into my life, please take care of him. Thank you for watching over me and my baby."

A noise came from the stairs. The scratch of nails on the metal treads. I grabbed a knife from the duffel bag and held my breath. The sound of scraping sped up. My sweaty hands clasped the knife in front of me.

A dog bound up the last step and ran to my side. His tail and tongue wagged in tandem as he sat up and begged with a low whine.

I fell over on my butt, a deep sigh escaping my lips. Just a dog.

I reached out and patted his head. "Sorry, dog. No food tonight."

He lied down and put his head on my lap. "I bet you were somebody's beloved pet." The Border collie closed his eyes and fell to sleep. I ran my fingers over his tangled fur and found a worn collar with a nametag. "At least I won't have to call you dog."

"Nickie," I whispered as I read the tag by the light of the Moon. My shaking fingers went to my lips and tears fell down my cheeks. Looking to the stars and the heavens above, my heart clenched in my chest and took my breath away. Someone was helping me. Someone was watching over me, over us.

"Thank you. Amen."

♦ ♦ ♦

"God, you don't have to help me, but it would be really fucking great if you didn't get in my way," Seth cursed for the hundredth time as the undead just kept coming. His truck would have been great right about now. Just when they'd cleared the area around a car, a horde would descend on them from nowhere.

"We wouldn't be doing this," he yelled over to Miranda and Cody. "If you weren't so damned determined to get to Brentwood, we could be safe in an apartment somewhere. With stairs."

He took a deep breath and plunged a machete into the face of the skinbag in front of him. After the heat of the summer they all looked alike. Like something six months in the grave, except they were walking and killing. The zombie fell and another half dozen took its place.

"Safe is surviving. Safe isn't living," Miranda yelled right back.

Man, the girl had a mouth on her. This was the girl he remembered from his supply runs to the compound. Finding a friend her own age had helped the healing process a thousand times more than he'd been doing. Ran had become a mini-Emily. A zombie hunter extraordinaire.

The kids stepped in close and guarded his back. They made a great team if he did say so himself. Why did they need anyone else? Cody answered his unvoiced question.

"Security in numbers, dude. If there is a

group, we should, like, join it."

He smiled at Cody's surfer slang voice. His smile slipped as a once-male undead shambled up to him. The cargo shorts and skateboard-logoed shirt matched his young companion's outfit. With a grimace he yelled, lunged, and then sent the blond-haired head flying with a swipe of his blade.

Taking a cautious look around, he listened to blessed silence. Bending, he wiped the blood from the machete on the shirt of the fallen and put it back in the sheath.

"Keep an eye out, guys," he mumbled as he opened the car door and sat in the front seat. The keys were still in the ignition. A few grinding turns, and a lot of stomping the gas pedal, and the motor turned over. It purred like a kitten. The luxury car lived up to its expensive hype. Built for comfort and durability. They cruised down the middle of the street, and knocked zombies out of the way, with three-quarters of a ton of Detroit's finest.

Seth tuned out the kids chatter as they rambled on as only the young know how to do. Hours of talking with nothing said. His mind turned inward. Gritting his teeth, he knew if it were up to him they would be going anywhere but back to Brentwood, a town with nothing for him.

"Okay," Cody said over his shoulder, reaching and turning on the radio. Miranda leaned forward, a smile on her face as the young man spun the dial.

"There hasn't been anything on the air for

months, Ran," he managed to say just before a voice came on over the air. A shiver spiked down his spine. Like a reminder of all they had lost, a sexy DJ voice came on and spoke.

"The Bay Area's Best is back on for another night of rocking and rolling, friends. After a hard day of fighting the undead and fearing the bad and the mad of society let's unwind and relax with some Blue Oyster Cult."

A click sounded on the radio and the well-known strains of *Don't Fear the Reaper* filled the car and his head. Seth started laughing so hard he had to stop the vehicle in the middle of the freeway and hold his sides.

If the zombie apocalypse could have a theme song, that would be it.

Jill James

CHAPTER TWENTY-ONE

The road doesn't get any harder, but it doesn't get any easier.
Every stranger is friend or foe, decided in an instant.
Trust is a commodity no one can afford.
— Seth Ripley

A squeal of the brakes and the jerk of the car yanked Seth out of a dead sleep in the passenger seat of the car. He peeled his eyes open to bright morning sun and wanted to close them again. K-rails barricaded the freeway in front of them. Turning his head, he glanced for a way around that wasn't appearing. The concrete rails spanned the whole eight lanes. The hillsides went straight up on either side of the freeway. K-rails blocked the off-ramp as well.

Things went from bad to worse, which is the only way things could go in the zombie apocalypse, he thought yet again. A giant stepped from behind the barrier with a B.F.G. Otherwise known as a big, fucking gun. The man made it look like a toy with his bulging biceps and enormous head sitting on no neck.

A quick glance at Cody and Miranda showed a young man ready to shit his pants and a girl ready to die of shock. He sucked in air and grabbed the AR-15 at his feet. The man stood like a statue, the gun not fired yet, but still pointed at their windshield.

"Enough of this shit," he muttered under his breath. "I'm tired of zombies. I'm tired of people who don't think zombies are bad enough. I'm tired of being tired."

Easing the door open, he pulled himself out of the car. The lone sentinel still stood at attention. Seth moved away from the vehicle hoping the gun would follow him and stay away from the kids. He gulped with a dry throat as his hopes were fulfilled. The gun looked even larger when he stared down the bore. A dark hole of death looking much bigger than it was.

The man's black skin shone in the sunshine brightening the sky. His shoulders wouldn't have looked out of place on an Oakland Raiders linebacker. His dark eyes stared at Seth with a glare that meant business.

Moving his arm slightly, Seth pulled the gun back and pointed it in a hopefully non-threatening direction. He took a deep breath as the large man hefted the weapon to his shoulder.

"We don't want any trouble. We're just traveling through," Seth said.

"You can't go through without paying the toll," the man's voice rumbled like rocks in a cement mixer. "Nobody goes through without paying."

A glance in the near distance showed blood-splattered vehicles sprawled across the concrete roadway. No zombies shambled across the freeway, so the man appeared to be giving mercy headshots.

The man's stare turned on Cody and Miranda and hairs rose on Seth's neck. His hand twitched on the trigger of his gun when the stare centered on Miranda. He raised the gun.

"We don't have much, but we can spare some food and water."

"Don't need food or water, got plenty. Some things I don't have," he rumbled, still staring at Miranda.

"Not. Going. To. Happen," Seth gritted out

between clenched teeth.

The man's head whipped toward Seth and a grin split his face. A bright-white slash against his ebony skin. In an instant, his whole demeanor changed. The ominous man became a gentle giant with the grin of a little boy on his face.

"Oh, no. Don't mean that little girl," he said. "Hoping you got some chocolate and soap. Maybe some razor blades, but that is probably hoping too much. Hoping doesn't get you much anymore, does it?"

"What about them?" Seth jerked his chin toward the shot up cars. "Did they not have any chocolate?"

The man pulled the gun off his shoulder and rested the stock on the ground. He took off his baseball cap and ran a forearm over his bald head. "Don't know about any chocolate. Ain't looked yet. I do know that they came with guns blazing, no questions asked. Nobody shoots at Teddy Ridgewood and gets away with it." He put the cap back on his head and held out his hand to shake.

Seth moved closer and reached out. His hand was enveloped in the large, black one. They shook a few times and Teddy's smile grew. "Teddy Ridgewood or you can call me the King of Pittsburg. Ruler of a dead town."

"Seth Ripley. The kids are Cody and Miranda. I kind of inherited them."

He waved and the young man and woman got out of the car and strolled over. Teddy shook hands and introduced himself. Seth kept watch as the trio talked and laughed when the man again said he was King of Pittsburg.

"Where are the skinbags?"

"The what?" Teddy asked.

"The undead. The zombies." Seth replied, listening to the silence of the town.

"Aren't any. All gone. All the people gone, too."

"How can there be none?" Miranda asked before he could. She had her neck craned back, staring up at the enormous man.

"Well," Teddy began. "Most of the people died of the flu. Town was down to a couple thousand. Then the dead started not staying dead, and we lost a bunch of people that way. So when the crazy people came through and collected the ones I had, I ended up with just me. I've looked all over. I'm the only one left."

"That was General Peters and his group. The crazy people coming through," Miranda spit out. "I was with them. They have a way to control the horde. Can make them come and go where they want."

"You don't say," Teddy said. "Well, ain't that the darnedest thing. Trained zombies."

It looked as if Miranda wanted to say something more, but before she could get a word out Cody grabbed her hand and the tension left her shoulders and she smiled.

"We're headed to Brentwood. There a group there. The general, all his people, and the zombies were going to attack them." Seth rubbed the back of his neck. "Been ten days; two weeks maybe."

"That sounds about right. I think that's when I heard the people come through here," Teddy said, hefting his big gun back onto his shoulder. "After that, I put up the barricades. Figured if I'm going to be king, I should get something for people going through my land."

The big man laughed until tears poured down his face. Then he sobered up. "It's kind of lonely being king of nothing. You folks can stay if you want."

Seth looked around. It seemed a nice place but one glance at Ran's stubborn face said she was having nothing to do with stopping before they got to their destination.

"Ran, you know General Peters might be in charge when we get there. The three of us can't take him on."

Her brow furrowed. "I'm not living my life looking over my shoulder all the time. If we get there and he is in charge, we can find more people until we have enough to fight back. Don't you care what happened to Emily?"

"Of course I care," he shouted. "But seeing it isn't going to help. It will make it worse. Like this world can get any worse."

"It'll help me," Ran whispered, her hand clenched into a fist. "That bastard will pay."

As if he could read the young woman's mind

and see her troubles painted on her face, Teddy reached over and patted her shoulder. "Yes he will."

Seth threw his hands up in the air. He could tell when he was outnumbered. "I guess we are going to Brentwood."

"Yes," Teddy said, bumping fists with Miranda and Cody. "I've always wanted to live in the country."

The man started walking toward the K-rails blocking the off-ramp. He waved them to their car and directed them to back up and head to the ramp. Teddy strode to the top and disappeared, to return with a tow truck to move the rails.

Miranda laughed in the back seat of the car. "I thought he would just pick them up and move them."

Cody and Seth joined in the laughter. "I'm pretty sure even Teddy couldn't move them without a few more guys." He put the car into drive and followed the tow truck once the man cleared the way.

"Why are there no cars in the road?" Miranda asked, her head swiveling back and forth. "Everyone is parked and out of the way."

"If I had to guess, I'd assume Teddy moved them to make it easy to drive up and down the main street here."

Seth looked all around. "Sure you don't want to stay? Nice town. No zombies."

She shook her head. "We are not staying."

"Dude, the Queen of California has spoken," Cody said with a bow of his head to Miranda.

They all laughed as they pulled up beside Teddy's tow truck in a parking lot in front of a marina. The boats bobbed in the gentle waves of the river, their shiny paint gleaming in the sunshine. Seth punched the steering wheel and sighed.

How could the world be so beautiful and so ugly at the same time? Somebody had a fucked sense of humor.

They got out of the car and grabbed weapons and backpacks of food and water. Teddy strolled down the pier, the wooden expanse wobbling back and forth with his weight. They followed as the big guy unlocked a gate and waved them through. He locked it behind them, and they all walked to the last boat.

Seth's breath caught in his throat and his heart pounded in his chest. The beat thrummed in his ears and his fingers tingled as he tried to keep a grip on his gun.

Teddy stepped aboard the boat with gleaming white paint and its name glittering in metallic blue. Emily. Yes, a fucked sense of humor, indeed.

◆ ◆ ◆

Getting woken up to a growling dog with the fur on his back standing up is not a good thing. Hearing the moans of the undead over the growling is even worse. I stood up and stretched. Metal was harder than rooftop to sleep on. On the other hand, I had been able to sleep with my canine companion on watch.

Yawning, I walked to the edge of the tank and stared at a dozen or so of the skinbags. The stench rolled over me and turned my stomach. My hand flew to my mouth and I swallowed the sour taste. Wanting to be pregnant was one thing; enjoying morning sickness was another thing entirely.

Nickie the dog stared over the edge as well, his growls in competition with the zombs. With rapid steps, I walked back to the duffel bag and picked up the digital recorder. A push of the button and the dog stopped growling and he sat up and stared at me. Looking over the edge again I smiled as the undead ran away as fast as their pitiful bodies could go.

I squatted and petted Nickie. "Let's see if we can find some people. Some good people." Standing, I scanned in the direction of The Streets and the Target center even further away. A chill swept over me as smoke rose in a gray pillar where the other shopping center should be.

Shaking my head, I gathered my few belongings. I wouldn't know what had happened unless I went there. The comfortable weight of the crossbow sat on my back as I grabbed the duffel bag and took the stairs in a careful speed. The dog followed at my side. Several times I had to scoot him aside with the edge of my foot. The sound from the recorder might scare zombies, but apparently it made a dog stick to me like glue.

Once Nickie and I came off the hill and back

to the road, I flipped off the recorder. Silence filled the early morning. A chill lingered as the sun rose across Brentwood. The brighter the light became, the more ominous the smoke became. Walking down the road, it was easier to see it was probably right where the shopping center I was heading to should be.

I wanted to curse the fates, but the dog rubbed against me and it wasn't hard to remember all I had to be thankful for—the baby, the escape from the general, and for Nickie. A present I was sure came right from Nick. Still being my partner, still having my back.

CHAPTER TWENTY-TWO

How could I hold on to my new-found faith when everything in the world seemed determined to show me how shitty it could be? The Target store and the group attached to it were gone. Squinting into the haze from the smoke, I spotted several people dead on the ground. I moved closer. No bites. Just burned skin and broken bones. They weren't burnt undead, just burnt dead. Something had killed them.

I brought my forearm up against my nose. The stench of burning oil and plastic roiled out of the shattered storefront to mingle with the sickening odor of burning flesh. A quick scan of the area showed no other damaged buildings. I squatted down and petted Nickie.

"I bet a propane tank or furnace blew. I don't think the zombie army came through here."

To my right, the sporting goods store stood unharmed except for scorch marks and other red, wet marks I didn't want to identify on the wall. A few skinbags meandered in front of it. I turned the recorder back on as I jogged over. They scattered like plastic bags blown across a parking lot.

Plywood filled the doors where the glass had been. Reaching out, I banged on the wood with my fist, waited a second, and then put my ear to the wood. Silence greeted me. I did it again. Still nothing.

I pulled a flashlight out of my duffel bag and went inside. The musty scent filled my nostrils. It felt empty, if a place is capable of feeling empty. I shut the door and turned back to the cavernous place. Like a strobe, I swung the light back and forth to see if anything jumped out at me. Thankfully, still nothing appeared.

I allowed myself a small sigh. Cockiness gets you killed in the ZA. I turned off the recorder. Batteries were the first order of business. Before, batteries filled the checkout lines. After wasn't much different. Except, the group had them all spread out on a table by the registers. A giggle escaped me. Shoplifting doesn't count if there was no one left to take your money.

I took all the double A's for the recorder and the D's for the flashlight. I left the rest. Someone else might come along and need them. Greed wasn't good in the ZA either.

Heading to the back where the crossbows and bolts were, I took a deep breath. Just dust. No decay. No rot. Like a girl in a jewelry store, I smiled when I spotted all the stuff left. Plenty of bolts for the crossbow, holsters for the guns, and even some ammo.

I found a backpack that fit well after trying on several and transferred most of the stuff over. Grabbing some protein bars and bottles of water gave me a sense of relief. Starvation and dying of thirst were too easy at the end of the world without the ease we were used to having instant food the minute we were hungry. Drive-thru fast food restaurants and easy microwave meals have spoiled us. The duffel bag got the extra ammo and some guns that I wasn't sure what they took but would make good trade goods. That would be my drop bag. The one I'd drop if I had to get the hell out of somewhere in a hurry. Food, water, and supplies were staying with me.

Loaded up, Nickie and I headed to the front. The scratching alerted me before we reached the doors. The odor confirmed it. Undead waited for us outside. I reached for the recorder and it wasn't in my pocket. In a panic, I swung in a circle. It wasn't on the battery table. It had to be back at the guns. A plywood panel cracked and popped off the door. Nickie yelped and started growling, his fur up on end. *Why does everything have to be so damned hard? All I wanted to do was go out the door I came in. Was that too much to ask for?*

"Come," I yelled, running back to the gun section. The recorder sat on top of the glass case where I'd stupidly left it. I scooped it up as I ran. A push of the play button brought no sound, nothing. Damn batteries. I stuffed it in my pocket and headed to the rear of the store. Exit doors are usually by the bathrooms. And those are usually in the right or left rear.

The crash of display cases and clothing racks filled the store. I swung the flashlight to the right. No bathrooms. Left it was then. We ran. The thump of my boots and the scratching of the dog's nails on the linoleum floor filled my ears.

The green light was dead with no power, but the Exit sign hung over the hallway. Slowing down, I took several deep gulps of air and held my breath. Chaos behind me, silence in front of me. The flashlight's beam picked out the silver bar on the emergency exit. No electricity, so I didn't need to worry about an alarm. No chains or locks on the door. I let out my held breath.

Moans and shuffling were getting closer. "Okay, Nickie. One. Two. Three."

We burst through the door and slammed it shut behind us. Looking around, I spotted a board and jammed it under the doorknob. I kicked the bottom as a thud sounded on the door, followed by several more. The handle rattled but the board held.

Pulling the gun from the holster, I turned in a circle. Nothing was there. I said a quick, silent prayer in my head. Ten seconds later I had reason to say a much longer one. In the corner of the enclosed back lot stood a bicycle with an attached baby trailer. I stopped to listen, nothing but the breeze carried to my ears. A price tag fluttered on the handlebar. Taking a moment, I heaved a huge sigh of relief. I wouldn't need to face a baby zombie or a zombie mommy. The thought would be funny if it wasn't so depressing or real.

When one door shuts, another one opens. Or in this case, an even better door opened. Someone was watching over me and I knew it. Knew it deep down inside.

In seconds, I had the backpack and duffel bag in the trailer with my crossbow. The gun and holster stayed on me. Now, all I had to do was find the first rendezvous spot. Commander Canida had made us memorize the location and several ways to get there. All I had to do was find Oakley and Neroly Road.

I'd tried to get Nickie into the trailer too but he wasn't having any of it. A few yelps and scratches on my arms convinced me to let him walk. I loaded the recorder with new batteries and put it in a fanny bag attached to the handlebars. I knew it was working, because my fillings hurt and the dog was right at my side again.

The familiar saying of never forgetting how to ride a bicycle is partially true. I hadn't been on one since childhood, and the trailer made me wobble a little, but a hundred yards down the empty, cracked asphalt brought it all back. By the time I reached the dead end and turned right on a small road, I was pedaling along.

I glanced at the department store sitting by itself in a field of waist-high weeds that had claimed the parking lot and wondered for the umpteenth time what Brentwood would have been like without the end of the world knocking it on its ass. The large store sat by itself. A huge sign by the freeway proclaimed more had been coming. A promise of prosperity frozen permanently in time.

The thump of the undead on the inside of the glass doors of the store had me pedaling faster.

Nickie easily kept up, his tongue lolling out of his mouth as he trotted by my side.

We stopped where the shopping center's street met the road. The silence was thick and heavy. No insects chirping. No birds calling to each other. Not even the bark of a dog. The town was dead in all ways.

The moan of a skinbag across the road caught my attention. He swayed back and forth, caught in the barbed wire strung in front of a house. Putting the kickstand down, I hopped off the bike and got a knife from the trailer. I strapped the sheath onto my belt and pulled the blade.

Skinbag was a relative term. There seemed very little skin left beyond a few hanging tatters. The rest had been seen to by carnivorous predators and rapacious birds.

The undead had been an elderly man judging by the gray hair clinging to the remains of his peeling scalp.

Putting my hand on his head, the blade of the knife slid into his temple with ease. The burning hunger died in his opaque eyes and his chattering chomping jaw fell silent as he sagged against the barbed wire. The metal strands pulled loose from the wood posts and he collapsed to the ground.

I stepped back, fell to my knees, and burst into tears. Dry heaves brought up bile and not much else.

The tears died and my stomach calmed. I'd never been pregnant before but I'd read enough books in my fruitless quest to recognize hormone swings and hunger pangs had me in a dangerous state. I couldn't remember my last food beyond the orange from Antonio.

Harshly wiping my cheeks, I cleaned the knife on the zomb's shirt and jammed it back into the sheath on my belt.

I glanced across the road to see Nickie sitting at attention beside the bike.

"Okay, buddy. Water, food, and we hit the road."

I shot a look up and down the street as I jogged back to the bike. A quick search in the backpack yielded a bottle of water and a protein bar I'd grabbed and thrown in at the sporting goods store. Using my hand as a cup, I shared half of the water with Nickie, as well as the hard as a rock granola bar. Good thing their expiration date was years from now, because I was starving and being stale wasn't going to stop me.

My stomach grumbled as food and water reached its emptiness. I held my breath, but the contents seemed willing to stay put. The dog looked up at me with pleading eyes, but the moans of zombs on the move had me pushing him away and straddling the bike.

With a tap of my boot heel, the kickstand was up and we were again on our way. To the north and the next town over should be the survivors of the attack on the compound, if there were any. I crossed my fingers and sent a quick prayer skyward, because if they weren't there, the second site was a whole hell of a lot more miles away.

Before I knew it, we hit Neroly Road. At a crossroads, the flat land was deserted. The middle of nowhere, rolling tumbleweeds punctuating the point. A few houses sat back from the road, but no live people appeared. The breeze carried dust and the tumbleweeds down the middle of the road, looking so much like a movie of the apocalypse as to be surreal. I sat there a moment waiting for the gang from Mad Max to come thundering up the road.

I wiped the grit from my eyes and pushed off. The dog stayed by my side. Sometimes I had to swerve to miss his paws, he was so determined to be right under my feet, but in the middle of unfamiliar territory I was leaving the recorder on as long as possible.

Coming around a curve, we came upon houses. I pedaled slower. Red X's marked the doors of each home. Some had shattered or boarded-up windows. What had been once verdant lawns sat brown and dead, weeds grew waist-high to the edge of front windows. Some had burned down to the foundations. The feel of a ghost town followed me as I pedaled down the middle of the road, allowing ample room for unpleasant surprises.

I stopped the bike and trailer with a skid. The RV storage yard sat a few burned-to-the-ground houses up the street. People bustled in and out of the front gate. I spotted several kids I didn't know, but a big red R-1 graced the cinderblock wall and the American flag flew overhead.

I looked down at the dog. Tears burned my dusty eyes. "We found them, Nickie." Now, I wasn't alone.

"Emily," a female voice yelled from on top the wall.

I waved as Michelle jumped down from the wall and ran toward us.

CHAPTER TWENTY-THREE

Darkness only masks the evil on the land.
Flowing water only conceals the moans.
Nothing escapes the rot of the dead who refuse to die.
— Seth Ripley

The soft whispers and the occasional giggle from Miranda filtered from the cabin below, up to the deck. Seth rubbed his aching phantom fingers and pushed his gloved hand away in disgust. The smile on the young woman's face as she'd gazed at Cody had made it easy to retreat up the stairs to join Teddy in fishing.

A pile of flapping fish in a bucket brought back the memory of taking the first load of fish to the Brentwood shopping center. His breath caught. The day he'd met Emily. His first glance of her as she battled zombies from atop a truck. Her soft dark hair cut short, framing her lovely face. Her dark eyes shining bright and full of life. Her happy acceptance of the life she now had. One that was not even close to the one before. Her tears and anger at young Nick's senseless death.

He rubbed his chest. It hurt, deep inside, to think of Emily's spirit crushed by the relentless undead army at General Peters' beck and call. Pinching the bridge of his nose, still the tears came.

A large hand thumped on his back. "You lost someone special, didn't you?"

Special? Yes, Emily had been that. That and more. "Her name was Emily. She was the fiercest fighter I've ever seen. The bravest woman I've ever met."

Teddy's eyes narrowed. "Did you see her die? Did you have to...you know?"

His gaze focused on the sunlight bouncing off the river. "No, I wasn't there. But General Peters and his zombie army were headed there after the attack at the hospital in Concord. There's no way the people at the shopping center could have won against a force that big. The hospital fell in minutes according to Miranda."

"Believe half of what you see and none of what you hear," Teddy said, grabbing his jerking fishing pole and reeling in the line.

Seth laughed. "Where did you get that pithy saying?" His fishing pole jerked in its holder and he reached out to get it before it went overboard into the river.

Teddy reeled in his fish, pulled it off the hook, and tossed it into the bucket. He leaned the pole against the side of the boat. "My momma would say that anytime I said someone said something about someone else. That woman didn't hold with any gossip at all. She wouldn't even read those magazines at the store checkout line. She said they were for people who didn't have enough to worry about in their own lives, so they had to butt into others."

Teddy turned in a circle, rocking the whole boat. "Lot of good it did us. Worrying about who Brad Pitt was dating or who wore what to which award show didn't stop all this, did it?"

Seth sat back, his fishing pole forgotten in his hand. "What does Brad Pitt have to do with the end of the world?"

The big man spread his arms wide. "As far as you can see. That is all we have. No more 24/7 cable news. No emergency broadcasts. No more telling us every detail whether we need to know it or not. Nothing to tell you the shopping center and its people were overrun or not. No 'breaking news' to show the outcome. No telling if your Emily is dead or alive. But you won't know until you get there."

"I don't need to see her shuffling around as the undead to know she is gone," Seth got out in a loud, cracked voice. "I know she's gone. In here." He thumped his chest. "I'm not going to Brentwood."

"Miranda, stop!" Cody yelled over the thump of the girl's boots.

She burst through the door and onto the deck. "You promised," she cried, pointing at Seth as he stood. She walked over until her finger pressed against his chest. "You promised."

He pushed her hand away. "Promises don't mean anything anymore. Nothing means anything anymore."

The girl pulled her knife from its sheath and had it at his temple before he could take a breath. "Just say the word. I'll put you out of your misery. But you'll leave this world never knowing. Is that what you want?"

His breath left him in a shudder as he pushed Miranda's knife away and fell into the deck chair. Did he want to die? He could join his mother and Emily in death. He closed his eyes. The boat rocked and the dark comforted. A million pictures flashed across his mind in the second from one breath to the next.

Of her baking cookies when he was a little

boy, the warm scents of chocolate chip goodness filling their home. Of her cool hands on his forehead when he was sick. Of taking her to the hospital when the zombie virus hit.

A flash and he was with Emily in her tent. Touching her silky skin with his fingertips was as real as life. Her cries of passion during their love-making echoing in his brain and even her cries of anger when he'd left filling him with shame.

His eyes shot open. "No. I don't want to die yet. But if we find her as one of the undead at the shopping center, I will release her to the final death by myself. Are we understood?"

Ran and Cody nodded at his question. Teddy looked away and pretended to be fishing even though the line wasn't in the water.

Seth turned to the big man. "You'll watch over them, won't you?"

"Of course," the man's voice rumbled like thunder in a rainy sky.

Miranda stared at him, tears falling down her face. "I don't understand."

He grabbed her hands and held them. "I'll go back. I'll see what is there. Prove that Emily is dead. Then we will go our separate ways. You have Cody now. Teddy will watch over you both."

Her hands squeezed tightly. "Then that? You'll kill yourself?" Her voice cracked.

Seth pulled his hands back, looked away, and didn't say a word.

♦♦♦

By the time darkness was falling, Teddy had the boat ready to go. They'd eaten the fish dinner in silence. Miranda wouldn't look him in the eye and her tears still fell from time to time. Cody held her hand and she leaned on him.

They gathered round as Teddy took the wheel and ordered them to cast off and to secure stuff. The man acted as if he knew what he was doing, so Seth just followed orders, pulled the rope from the pier, and gathered it into a looping pile on deck.

"You seem like you've done this a few times. Have you?" he asked as Teddy navigated the boat away from the dock.

"Oh, sure. This was my uncle's boat. We went out every weekend from the time I was a little boy." Seth stared up at the giant and Teddy laughed. "Yes, at one time I was little."

"So what's the plan?"

"You want to go to Brentwood. We'll get to the Antioch Bridge first. We'll dock there and follow the highway into town. Easy, peasy."

"I doubt anything is easy anymore," Miranda piped up as she and Cody joined them at the wheel.

"Not easy, but doable with the four of us," Seth said, wrapping his arm around Ran's shoulders and relaxing as she let him.

The full Moon came up with a brisk breeze blowing from the river to the land. The light shone over the ripples of water, breaking and glimmering.

The wind carried the freshness of the river and covered the stench of the undead on land. The moans were muffled and then died as the boat floated along the water highway. The tension left his shoulders.

"How long will it take?" Miranda asked Teddy.

"Well, we have to go slow because it's dark and I can't use the lights. In the old days, it would take no time at all to go the distance to the bridge. But at our putting along, I'd have to say about two hours, maybe."

Seth felt the tension in Miranda's shoulders. "How far to Brentwood?"

"About five or six miles, give or take."

She smiled.

"But we have to anchor at the bridge and wait for daybreak."

Her smile fell. "Why can't we go as soon as we get there? Six miles is two hours, even walking slow."

"Don't know about you, Miss Miranda. But Teddy is not walking through zombie land in the dark," Teddy said, his eyes forward, his hands on the wheel.

"Damn," her voice broke. "I just want to get there."

"And we will," Seth spoke up. "In one piece."

"Fine." She flounced over to a seat like the teenager she still was as she threw herself down on the cushion. "But we leave at first light."

"Yes, ma'am," Teddy answered.

He held his laughter in as Teddy's enormous shoulders shook with his own silent laughter.

Just as the big man promised, in a couple of hours the bridge appeared like a dinosaur arched over the river. In the dark, with just the light of the Moon it could have been a brontosaurus come to the river for a drink.

"Dude," Cody spoke up. "I'm waiting for the music from Jurassic Park to start playing."

Miranda laughed. "Lots of people said it looked like a dinosaur."

Seth had to agree.

They drifted into its shadow in the middle of the river. Teddy pushed a button and the sound of the anchor clattering filled the air. It stopped suddenly and silence reigned again.

Teddy turned from his seat at the wheel. "You should have seen the old bridge, before this one. All wood and old. It creaked and moaned when you went across in your car. Felt like it swayed too."

Seth shuddered. He'd always hated bridges. The thought of it breaking and sending him to a watery grave had filled many childhood nightmares and made his first days as a truck driver harder than they'd had to be.

"I'll take first watch," he volunteered, turning his arm to look at his missing watch, a habit he hadn't had time to break yet. He kept meaning to get a new one after losing the last one fighting a zombie, but some other aspect of survival always took precedence.

"It's nine thirty now," Teddy said, looking at his own watch.

"How do you know it's right?" Miranda asked before he could.

"Synced to the Atomic Clock in Colorado, which I assume has to be running at least for a little while longer. Plus I check it at noon every couple of weeks."

"Cool," Miranda and Cody intoned together.

"Seth and I will take the first watch," Teddy said. "You kids can take over at two. By five thirty, six o'clock should be close to dawn. I'd feel better if we watched in teams."

Miranda and Cody nodded and headed down the stairs to below deck. Seth didn't buy the team story Teddy was handing out. The man meant to convince him to live.

Wasn't going to happen.

CHAPTER TWENTY-FOUR

"You can't leave. You just got here," Michelle said, tapping her foot and giving me the 'I'm serious' look.

"I've been here for two days. I'm not leaving. I have to go back to the shopping center. I know my necklace is there somewhere," I replied, my fingers reaching for it like the phantom pain of a missing limb. The only thing I had left of my parents and my old life that I cared about.

"Why can't you wait for Canida to get back? He could send you with a few of his men."

I yanked on the 'purse' I'd made for the tape recorder with the zombie repel sound to keep my hands free to fight. A copy of the sound was now with Jed Long. He'd managed to practice some with variations to test on the zombies nearby, few though they were. The signal was working to keep the area clear.

"At least take some RVers."

I stared at her and tossed my crossbow to

my back. "They're a bunch of kids. The oldest is maybe twelve."

She put her hand on my arm. "Age doesn't matter anymore and you know it. They've managed to survive here for three months after all the adults died. They've held this place all on their own."

I patted her hand and moved it from my arm. "Nickie and I will be fine. It'd take an hour or two to get there, barring any difficulties. No more than an hour to look around. Then I'll head on back. I'll be here in time for dinner."

"I wish I could go with you," she said, her arms hugging her body.

"Well, you can't. You have responsibilities now, Mom."

She smiled, her gaze traveling over the paved blacktop, spotting her new clan running, playing tag, a group of young orphans who had adopted my friend.

"Now all you need is someone to play daddy with you."

Her smile died. "Not yet. I can't."

I wrapped my arms around her and hugged her tight. "Don't wait too long or all the good ones will be taken."

She laughed and lightened the mood. "It's not like there is a large selection to start with."

Grabbing her hand, I dragged her to the front of the RV storage yard. I pushed the button and the gate rattled and slid open. Someone had rigged it to only open enough for a person to walk through. I stood outside with Nickie as Michelle pushed the button and the gate rattled and slammed shut.

Electricity via solar panels, water from wells dug in the yard, and comfortable beds in the RVs stored there before the apocalypse. What was I doing going back to the Streets mall to look for a useless trinket? For something that had nothing but sentimental value in this new world. But my gut said I needed it. I needed to go back and see what was left in the daylight. I needed to go today.

A whimper caught in my throat. My gut also told me to go back and bury Seth or at least the dead zombie I thought might be Seth. If there was a chance it was him, the father of my unborn child deserved at least that much.

A hundred feet down the road I spotted some skinbags shambling aimlessly in circles. "We need to tell Jack and Jed that it seems to work to this point," I whispered to the dog as I reached into my bag and switched on the recorder. As soon as I pushed the button, the undead ran off like children from the Bogeyman. Jed needed to tweak the sound; it wasn't exactly the same as the one Antonio had given me.

Birdsong filled the air as the dog and I strode down the road. The other sounds were missing. All the background sound you get so used to in life was gone. No voices of children playing. No screeching of brakes or revving of motors. How quiet had this rural area been before the world died? There must have been the sound of radios and televisions, of neighbors talking while they took out the trash. The houses weren't so far apart that you couldn't have heard a mother calling her children to dinner.

At the intersection I pulled my crossbow off my back and fitted a bolt into the slot. The sound on the recorder would repel dead men but it did nothing for the live ones meaning to cause trouble. That's where the crossbow came in handy.

I'd barely taken two steps when the sound of a car motor filled my ears. I moved off the street into the shadow of an overgrown tree and weed-infested yard. A white minivan zipped around the corner and stopped. Hiding was futile, I'd been seen. Moving out of the shadows slowly, I walked to the sidewalk, Nickie at my side.

The window on the minivan rolled down and Suzy Soccer Mom leaned out the window. I brought the crossbow up to face her. Her mouth dropped open, her eyes went wide, and her hands shot up into the air. Empty hands. Taking a deep breath, I stood my ground.

"Who else is in there with you?"

"My son is driving and Melanie is in the back."

Leaving the motor running, the driver opened his door and came around the front of the vehicle. His head barely cleared the hood. His hands were up as well. The young mom got out and slid the side door open. A baby sat in a car seat in the back. Her blonde hair was dirty and tangled over her eyes.

I had a clear view and there was no one else

in the vehicle. I lowered the crossbow slightly.

"What are you doing out here?"

"Can I put my hands down?"

I nodded and waited. Everyone had a story and you had to decide instantly whether it was the truth or not.

"We were living in an old house down the road. Our food was getting low three days ago so my husband went out. He didn't come back," she finished with a sob and a hiccup. The young boy behind her rubbed his eyes and tears ran down his face.

"Where are you headed?"

"Some men found us at the house and told us to go to the RV storage yard. He said there were people there and safety. The guy said his name was Jack."

I lowered the crossbow to my side. "That's Commander Canida. He's our leader. Just continue down this road about half a mile and the yard will be on the right-hand side. Tell them Jack and Emily sent you."

The young mom smiled and her whole face brightened. "Can we give you a ride there?"

"Thanks, but I'm headed the other way. I'll be back tonight. Hope to see you there."

She whispered 'thank you' and they hopped back into the minivan and headed down the street.

I squatted next to Nickie. "Sometimes you meet the good ones. We have to collect all of them we find."

♦ ♦ ♦

It felt like Seth's head just hit the pillow and someone was shaking him to get up. Sunlight streamed through grimy windows. He sat up and wiped the sleep from his eyes. Finding his gloves, he slid them on fast, looking away as he pulled the special fitted one over his mutilated hand.

Miranda smiled at him. "You slept like a rock. Me, too. The rocking boat was like being in a hammock or a cradle. I haven't rested like this in months."

He smiled back. "Any breakfast? I'm starving."

The young woman headed to the stairs, calling over her shoulder, "Teddy caught some more fish this morning and found some oranges in his supplies."

He stretched and pulled on his shoes as Miranda's steps faded to above decks. Faint voices filtered down the stairs from the open door. Laughter had him hurrying with the shoe tying. With some practice he was almost as good as before losing his fingers.

On deck he was greeted with the delicious scent of frying fish and the deep timbre of Teddy's laugh drowning out Miranda's girlish giggles and Cody's chuckles.

"You were right, Miss Miranda," Teddy said. "The idea of oranges got his lazy butt up here in no time."

His smile fell. "You lied? My mouth was

watering just thinking about it."

Miranda laughed and pulled her hands out from behind her back. "Yep, no oranges. We have oranges *and* apples."

Seth eyed the orange and red fruit and smiled, almost tasting them. Strange how priorities could change with the end of the world as they knew it. He'd heard his mother's stories of growing up as a kid on the East coast and how an orange for Christmas was a treat. Before the time of international shipping and having fruit all-year round. Because it was summer somewhere in the world and the fruit came from Peru and Australia.

He took the orange from Miranda's hand and brought it to his nose. The pungent scent filled his nostrils and flooded his mind with good memories of summer days and easier times.

"May as well enjoy them. Probably the last we'll see for a while."

"Dude, you're being a killjoy. Perfect way to bring down the mood," Cody said, putting an arm around Miranda's shoulders. "Still orchards. Just won't have them year-round anymore."

She smiled. "Don't worry. It's just Seth's way."

His eyes opened wide. Was it his way to be a downer? He hadn't always been. He'd believed there was a future. Zombies and rampaging armies kind of took the optimism out of life. Still, he could try for Miranda and Cody. It wasn't their fault this was the world they were stuck with now.

He glanced toward shore and turned back to

Teddy. "So where do we get off this boat ride?"

The big man flipped a fish in the pan. "We eat. Not sure what we may find on the way. Then I get us to a pier on the other side of the bridge."

"Sounds like a plan."

A short time later, Seth finished up and patted his full stomach. "Okay, so let's get to land and head on out before Ran stages a mutiny."

Teddy navigated the boat and in short order the pier came into view. The undead filled the end, pushing up against each other, their moans carrying over the water.

Seth stared as they got closer and the skinbags got more animated at the sight and probably smell of fresh meat. Talking about the smell, he covered his nose as the boat pulled in closer.

Miranda and Cody came from below with backpacks, filled with Teddy's supplies from the bulging look of them.

The boat motor stopped and Teddy patted the wheel in what looked like a good-bye. "Not sure we'll make it back. The Emily's been a good boat. I'll miss her."

Seth craned his neck and looked up at the zombie-filled pier. "Now what?"

The man pointed to the opposite side of the boat. "Over the side. Water's gonna be a might cold, so no yelling. We walk from here."

Cody helped Miranda over the side. The frigid water came up to her thighs. He could see her holding her squeals in. Cody jumped in beside her.

"Not so bad, Dude," he called up to Seth.

He lowered himself over the side. Definitely cold, but bearable and barely knee height. He started walking to shore as he pulled the machete out of its holder. A big splash flung drops of water on him as Teddy fell in the river behind him.

Seth stumbled up the rocky shore and waited for Teddy. The zombs remained down at the end of the pier like they were too brain-dead to know how to turn around. They just kept pushing on each other. Someday the railing would give and they would tumble in like lemmings off a cliff. Teddy stumbled up beside him and shook himself like a wet dog.

"That wasn't too bad at all," the big man said, laughing.

"Speak for yourself, King Teddy," Miranda said. "My toes are frozen."

Teddy looked up at the sunny sky. "Be warm today. We'll be dry in no time. Bet you're sweating by the time we get to where you want to go."

She was stomping her feet. "I sure hope so."

"Behind you," Seth yelled as the first undead reached them from the parking lot. "Yep, sweating in no time," he muttered as Cody and Miranda went back to back and Teddy did the same for him. They spread out slightly and in a short time the ground was littered with the finally dead and the way was clear for their trek.

CHAPTER TWENTY-FIVE

"I spy something red and white," Miranda said, playing the classic game with Cody. The walk gone by faster than Seth had expected. He wasn't sure whether that was a good thing or a bad thing.

"That Coca-Cola can by the suitcase," Cody answered.

Teddy shook his head. "Do you think this will ever end or will future generations see something like a soda can and think it is an ancient artifact?"

Seth stared down at his boots and the broken asphalt, the cracks filled with weeds and plants. His ears picked up no sounds but Miranda's soft voice and the trudge of their boots.

"I think this is it," he replied. "Sure, the skinbags running around now will decay and fall apart. But if even one zombie is left alive, this starts all over again. Even then, we all have the virus, so we would need a cure for that too. Things will never be the way they were."

"That's a pretty sad vision for the world you

got there, don't you think?"

"How else can it be? The flu killed billions first. Doctors, scientists, planners, and visionaries had to be in that group. Then the dead rose and attacked millions more. What are the odds that the people who could fix this are still alive? What are our odds if they aren't that a next generation will have the knowledge and ability to fix it? Hell, the next generation will just be surviving, not figuring out quantum physics, the wonders of the DNA strand, or the cure for AIDS or cancer. In two or three generations we could be back to living in caves and oohing and aahing over fire."

"Man." Teddy sighed. "Just kill me now."

Seth slapped him on his giant bicep. "That my friend is the reason for my happy outlook on life."

Teddy gave him a slap back on his arm and almost knocked him over. "Thanks for the sarcasm, but I'm going to stay optimistic. Humans have a way of bouncing back, no matter what. We gotta have hope. Or we wouldn't keep having babies."

"Babies." He shuttered. He could still remember Emily's words when they'd discovered Beth, Nick's girlfriend, had been pregnant. She'd been so right to believe it was insanity to bring a baby into this world. Hell, it was insane for people to be in this world.

"Heads up, Dudes," Cody called back to them. "Three up ahead."

Fifty feet ahead stood three leather-covered

bikers of the undead. The one in the middle was almost as big as Teddy. He just laughed.

"I've got this."

He ran faster than his size would imply. Running smack into them, he sent them flying like bowling pins. One got up faster than the others and rushed Teddy. The big guy grabbed the zomb's head and twisted. The crack could be heard by Seth and the kids. He dropped him like a bag of trash. Walking over, he stomped his gigantic feet on number two's and three's heads and they lay still.

Teddy scraped the blood and guts from his shoes on the asphalt as he walked back their way. A big grin split his face. "Wow! I missed out being the king of an empty land."

"Seth," Miranda called out.

His head came up and he looked her way. She pointed an arm to the east. A small pillar of smoke rose from where he remembered a Target store being. Could they be another casualty of Peters and his zombie army?

He looked at her. Miranda nodded. "Okay, we should check it out. Someone could be hurt or they might know something about Peters."

Seth led the way off the freeway and across the field. They took the opening by the bookstore and came out in the enormous parking lot. He stopped and held up his hand. They all listened.

He heard nothing but birdsong and the wind. They continued to the blackened remains of the store. Miranda and Cody wandered about, kicking corpses and checking for live victims.

"Do you think this is the work of that Peters guy you were talking about?" Teddy asked.

Miranda came up to his side. "I don't think so. There's a lot more dead dead and just a few zombs. He uses the skinbags as suicide bombers. Body parts would be everywhere. Cody saw the side of the building and it looks like it blew up. Bricks and stuff hit the street and another store on that side. Maybe a furnace exploded or something."

His head shot up at the sounds of moans coming from the sporting goods store next to Target. Several undead spilled from the storefront, tripping over busted boards. Weighing the benefits of searching for supplies and making a hasty escape, he chose escape. He waved his hands to get Cody back to his side.

"Let's get back on the road and head to the shopping center."

"I thought this was the shopping center," Cody said.

"Nope, it's down the freeway another mile or so," Miranda answered him, grabbing his hand and pulling him along, swinging their arms as they went.

"Let's go kick some army butt."

Miranda said, "He isn't in the real army. He made it up to make him feel special."

"That is so wrong, Dudette. You got to earn that title."

Seth smiled as Miranda wrapped the young man willingly around her little finger. A small part of him missed her looking up to him like that, but a big part, the important part, knew this was how it was supposed to be. He could be assured that Teddy and Cody would look after her. Hell, Miranda would look after them right back.

As they approached The Streets shopping center, the west side looked great. He couldn't tell if they had fought and won or fought and lost. They strode further along the road and the damage on the front came into view.

Many of the buildings didn't exist anymore except as piles of rubble. The steel containers they'd used to block the streets were twisted, burned hunks of metal. They got to the overpass section of the road and hunkered down below the railings.

Seth shrugged off this backpack and dug out a pair of binoculars. Pulling them to his face, he scanned from one end of the complex to the other. It didn't look good. The field in front was cluttered with dead. The only promising sight was the distinct lack of any life at all. If the 'General' had overpowered the group, he wasn't in residence either. It looked safe enough to at least check out. Maybe they could discover what had happened from what was left.

◆◆◆

A quaint house stood on the corner with the required white picket fence to make it someone's dream come true. The dream was shattered by the pile of dead bodies in the front yard. The garage door stood open with burned rubber marks down the driveway.

I crept closer and saw all the skinbags were missing their heads. Commander Canida and crew had been through here, I would bet a chocolate bar on it. My stomach growled at the thought.

"Probably where the minivan came from," I told Nickie.

His ears perked up and his fur stood on end. The dog turned and barked at something behind me. That was the only warning I got as I turned and Tommy leaped on me and knocked me on my ass. I knew it was Tommy because what was left of his tiny T-shirt said so in bright blue letters.

His growl made my skin crawl as I shoved an arm under his chin to keep his few teeth from biting me. Either his zombification took them or he was the right age to want his two front teeth plus several more for a Christmas that wouldn't come for him.

I reached for my knife but my fingers weren't making it. I put both hands on his chest and shoved. The undead kid went flying as I sat up. The crack of his head hitting the curb echoed in the silent air.

Standing up, I pulled my knife and walked over to the tiny corpse, but it wasn't needed. My breath caught as I slammed the knife back into the sheath. Tears blurred my vision as I stared down at someone's son. I said a prayer for him and hoped it was enough.

Pulling it together each time I had to kill

someone was getting harder and harder in my hormone-flooded state. Between the adrenaline rush when the kid attacked me and my remorse afterward, I was a mess.

I held my breath. The zombie kid attacked me. My teeth weren't hurting. Nickie wasn't glued to my side. With a shaking hand, I reached into my bag and pulled out the recorder. I started breathing again. The on button was popped up. I pushed it on again. A zing went through my teeth and Nickie crouched at my feet.

"Okay, buddy. We are all good to go."

The dog and I retraced our steps of a couple of days ago. Down Neroly Road until it met Empire and back to what was left of the Target store. The fire was down to smoldering and the gray smoke in the air was a bare wisp.

Moans and the crunch of glass alerted me to a few zombs hanging out at the sporting goods store. A click up of the volume of the recorder and they were scurrying away. Too bad we didn't have tanks or something. We could corral them all and be done with this mess.

Once they shambled far enough away, I turned the volume down, and rubbed my jaw. The sound really did vibrate through my fillings. I headed south out of the shopping center. The plan was to take Shady Willow Lane and hit The Streets from the east side instead of the west side and the highway I'd left on.

"I think that shot I heard was Antonio taking out General Peters, but we need to be sure, don't we, dog?"

We hiked past a giant church with a parking lot full of cars. A shiver went down my spine. My imagination could all too easily see rows and rows of the dead who hoped that religion was the answer to the zombie apocalypse. I didn't deny them the right to believe, I just always thought God was everywhere, not just in a building you showed up in once a week to talk to him.

I rubbed my stomach in a slow circle and smiled. God was in every miracle, not in a specific location at a specific time.

Nickie and I passed a school with zombie children behind the fenced-in play yard. As we moved closer, they scattered like nerds running from the bullies. I patted the bag holding the recorder as if it were a talisman against danger. I couldn't afford to get used to thinking the sound was total protection. I kept my head up and my senses alert.

We passed subdivisions full of eerie quiet. Most of these houses had belonged to the people who had made The Streets compound their new home. Most of them had died when it was overrun by Peters and the zombie army. We were down to twenty-five or thirty people, plus the kids who had already made the RV yard their home.

The sun came out from behind a cloud and warmed my face, and as easily as that, brightened my mood. You had to enjoy every moment. Too bad it took this to make me see that. Why didn't I enjoy the sunshine on the bay back then? Why didn't I walk on the wharf and listen to the sea lions and feed the gulls? Why did I think the next charity ball was more important than just enjoying life, living in the moment?

"Come on, Nickie," I said to the dog as we reached the end of the shopping center. The containers at this end still stood in place, but the buildings on either side were nothing but piles of rubble. Moans echoed on the other side.

I bit my bottom lip. *Leave the recorder on or turn it off and clear them out?* A decision was reached in a split second. If I were going to search for my necklace, I needed the place as safe as I could make it. I didn't need to think it was safe and have the recorder pop off again.

Reaching into the bag, I pushed the thing off. I swung the crossbow to my back and climbed the pile of stones and mortar. By the time I reached the top, the stench of undead hit me. I gagged and swung my bow back around.

Thunk.

Thunk.

Two down and one too close to get with a bolt. I swung the bow to the side and got my knife. A shove through his skull and the zomb hit the ground. Catching my breath, I held it and listened. Faint moans carried from down the mall road.

I wiped the blade on the zombie's shirt, put it back in the sheath, and swung my bow back around, fitting it with a new bolt. Grabbing the two bolts out of the undead, I wiped them and secured them on the crossbow.

Nickie padded along in front of me, his nails scratching slightly on the hard concrete sidewalk. I stopped at each storefront to listen and sniff.

"Most of the skinbags must have died," I whispered to the dog. "I think the buildings fell on them."

His ears perked up as if he understood me. I rubbed his head and we moved on. I stepped as quiet as possible, as Nick had taught me when I'd first arrived and we'd been paired up.

A knot formed in my throat seeing The Streets destroyed like this. This had been my home for six months, a safe haven, and the General and his zomb army had taken that away. I prayed that General Peters had gotten his just deserts.

CHAPTER TWENTY-SIX

Seeking justice darkens the soul.
Finding justice frees the soul.
Sometimes seeking and finding
is one and the same.
— Seth Ripley

"Come on, Seth," Miranda begged. "I don't see any movement. We didn't come all this way to just stand around and debate."

"He's just trying to keep you safe, Miss Miranda." Even in a whisper the man's voice rumbled like thunder.

She settled down and squatted next to him. "Do you see anything?"

He brought the binoculars down. Swallowing with a dry throat, he tried to put into words what he had seen. Nothing was coming. He handed the binoculars to Miranda.

She put them to her eyes and inhaled deeply. Her hand shook as she lowered them. "It looks like a battlefield. Like the pictures in my history book of the Civil War and the World Wars."

Teddy stood tall and started walking toward the lower road to get to the shopping center. He called back, "Let's see who won."

Seth stood and pulled his backpack back on, watching as Ran and Cody followed suit. They trotted after the big man and finally caught up to his long strides. He looked up at Teddy as the man pulled a rifle from his back and set off over the weed-infested field. The foliage seemed to have grown a couple of feet since the last time he'd been here.

The closer they got to the shattered buildings, the uglier got the scene. Moans of the undead grew louder. Teddy held his arms to stop them from walking any further. Seth moved to the man's side and looked down.

The muddy pit teemed with skinbags. The group's approach had set them off, skeletal arms reaching for the living flesh they could smell and hear. Teddy aimed his rifle into the hole, but Seth pushed the barrel down.

"Too noisy."

"If they're still in the hole, they probably aren't going anywhere," Miranda added in a hushed whisper.

Seth nodded and his gaze swept the field leading to the mall. Several more pits filled the field. Along with several small holes and scattered body parts, they painted a picture of preparations on The Streets group's part. They'd had some kind of warning of the attack.

Cody grabbed Miranda's hand and moved a few steps ahead of him and Teddy. The boy's back stiffened and he stopped in his tracks. He turned to Seth. "We don't want to go this way, Dude. I think I know what made the scrambled zombs."

Seth moved up beside them as Cody pointed at a green box in front of them a few paces. The words on it said, *Front toward Enemy*.

"I've seen those on the History Channel," Seth said. "I think they need a detonator, but let's go around, just in case."

The group stepped back and went around the pit of zombies to a clear area and made their way to the first damaged buildings. His chest hurt as he stared at what had once been a beautiful mall in a different time and sanctuary to so many in this time.

No sound filled the area in front of them. Seth led the way and stepped through the blasted and ripped container to the other side. The piles of dead and finally dead painted an ugly picture of a devastating fight. The group had been overwhelmed, but they'd continued to fight.

A body laid to his right. Her head and body had taken damage from flying debris, but he could still recognize Emily's friend, Bobbie. Her hand held a detonator. She'd given her life to stop Peters from taking their home, and perhaps allowed some to escape.

"Damn him," Seth muttered. When he found the General the man would join the dead.

"He's here somewhere, I know it," Miranda said, her head turning back and forth. "That stupid bus is still out front. They wouldn't leave it; it carried the speakers and Antonio's equipment."

"I don't hear anything, how can you be sure?" he asked the young woman.

That stopped her for a moment. "It's below our hearing, like dog whistles. If you have fillings, it makes them hurt, like when you scrape them with your fork."

They all stood still. "But I don't feel anything," she added.

Seth looked at Teddy. "Why don't we look around? Maybe they all died. We can hope. I'll take Miranda and you can take Cody and see if you find anything useful that we can carry away from here. If there were survivors maybe they left something to tell where they went."

The man nodded and put his hand on the young man's shoulder. They walked away and Seth followed Miranda as she started looking.

◆◆◆

"You sent Cody away so he couldn't see me go all 'vengeance is mine,' didn't you?"

Seth laughed and walked beside her. "No, I know this is important for you, so I want to be here for you, just like you were there for me after my mom died and I was bit."

Tears filled Miranda's eyes and she brought her hand up and brushed them away. "I didn't think you understood."

She caught her breath as Seth's eyes turned dark and bottomless. She'd never seen that look before and hoped to never have it turned against her.

"If it wasn't so important to you, I would gut Martin Peters and let him wander the Earth as a soulless corpse. What happens to him if we find him is up to you."

"Thank you." She hugged him and relaxed as he hugged her back. Her friend wasn't lost. He was still here. She had time to convince him to live.

"That building over there seems a little less damaged. If I needed a place to stay, that would be it," Miranda said, pointing a few storefronts down the sidewalk.

Glass and debris crunched underfoot as they

made their way inside the store. A closed door marked Storage led off the dusty hallway. Miranda reached over and put her hand on the doorknob. Seth's hand held her back. He leaned and put his ear to the wooden door.

He nodded and she turned the knob. She pushed harder as boards and rocks blocked the door's opening. Seth put his hands on the door and helped. The door opened wide and Miranda cried out.

The stench of blood, and death, and rot filled the room. Nothing moved except the flies attracted to the blood on the body slumped against the wall to her right. She brought her hand up to her nose and breathed through her mouth.

The hole in his temple and the gun in his hand told the story of his choice to not come back. She stared into his black, dead eyes and whispered a prayer for Antonio Gomez.

"Bastard," Seth whispered.

Her gaze whipped around to the gore-soaked mattress. She'd assumed it had been a fight scene, but what was left of Martin Peters pulled against the ropes holding his zombie body to the bed. His face remained intact, those cold eyes no less evil in opaque undeath. His teeth snapped behind the Duct tape across his mouth and his neck stretched in impossible contortions as he tried to reach human food.

Heat rose in her face. He'd destroyed her again. She couldn't kill him, he was already dead.

She couldn't finish him off, to do so would give him mercy she had no intention of giving.

She squared her shoulders and turned to Seth. "In the old world, I'd turn him in to the police for kidnapping and raping me and get justice that way. He'd be put away so he couldn't hurt others. In this world, I guess we have to do the same."

Miranda walked over to the mattress and the abomination on it. "Martin Peters. You will never hurt anyone again."

She pulled her knife and placed the point on his temple. Seth's hand came up and held hers.

"Let me do it," he whispered. "Walk away."

Stepping back, she gave the knife to him. Her eyes stayed glued to Peters as her friend shoved the knife through the monster's head and pulled it back out with a twist.

The teeth stopped chomping and chattering. The body stopped twisting and turning. Martin Peters was dead.

Walking away, Miranda fell to the ground as something grabbed her ankle. Make that someone. She rolled over, scooting back and pulling Tanya with her.

"Oh, hell no," she yelled, bringing her foot down on the woman's head and listening to the satisfying crunch of bone.

She yanked her foot away and felt Seth's hands under her arms pulling her up.

"Are you okay? She didn't bite you, did she?"

"No, I'm fine. I'm better than fine." She dusted her pants off. "The Evil King and his Wicked

Witch are dead."

Seth laughed. He turned to leave the room. "What's that?"

She looked where he pointed. Antonio's equipment was shattered and broken in the corner. "I guess he wanted to make sure nobody else could use it."

He gave a loud exhale and put his arm around her shoulders. "It's for the best. No one has the right to that much power."

She nodded, leaving the room without looking back.

Outside, they found Teddy and Cody with a few more things to add to their supplies.

"The place is, like, so empty," Cody said in his funny, surfer-dude way.

She ran over and hugged him. "Like, totally."

CHAPTER TWENTY-SEVEN

Two days.

Could it really only be two days since I'd been held captive here? The helplessness I'd felt was gone, just a bad memory to send shudders down my spine and to bring nightmares in the future. I touched my stomach.

I was okay.

The baby was okay.

That monster didn't win. I did.

Getting down on my hands and knees I searched the debris-strewn room I'd been held in. Dirt burrowed under my fingernails. I scraped my knuckles as I moved a large rock. Turning, I reached under the bed. Getting up on my knees, I ran my hands over the blanket on the cot.

Nothing. It had to be here.

I ripped the coverings off the cot and flung them across the room. The tinkle of metal against rock barely carried over the empty space, but I heard it. Jumping up, I rushed to the far wall. There it was. A little dented and the chain broke. My fingers shook as I grabbed it and rested it in the palm of my hand. My lucky necklace. I'd found it.

"Yes," I whispered and tucked the necklace, broken chain and all, into my pants pocket. A quick push of the button on the recorder in my bag and my ears hummed and Nickie bounded into the room to sit at my feet. His tongue and tail wagged.

"Let's get out of here. Okay?"

I wasn't going to borrow trouble. I'd come with a mission and I'd accomplished that. I'd meant to bury the zombie I'd thought might be Seth, but maybe I just needed to let it go. I could come back when I had more people with me and we could kill the undead and bury everyone then.

The dog heeled like a doggie school alumni as we left the broken store and came out on the sidewalk. I looked left and right. No skinbags. I would go back the way I'd come. It'd worked the first time. We crossed the small road and jogged to the garden area in the middle of the compound. I shrugged out of my backpack and put my crossbow down to get some squash and zucchini left on the plants when everyone evacuated so quickly.

I grabbed a couple and shoved them into my pack. Nickie started turning in circles and barking, butting me with his head. I jumped up and grabbed my bow, putting a bolt into it without thinking.

I stared around the plants and back the way we'd come but I couldn't see anything. I turned back as the dog continued barking, running a little bit away and coming back.

My breath froze and my heartbeat stopped in my chest. I'd been so stupid. Just because the sound kept the skinbags away didn't mean it worked on people, and right now four of them were standing as still as statues only fifty or so feet away.

The Black man stood head and shoulders above the three other men. I squinted. The small one might be a female, with hair even shorter than mine. A longer look confirmed it. Three men; one a giant, and one woman.

I couldn't place the blond guy or the female. But there was something familiar about the other guy. His dark hair was long and tangled, along with a scruffy beard. His eyes widened and he opened his mouth.

"Emily." His cracked voice carried across the distance.

My crossbow fell from my numb fingers and I ran across the grass before I knew I was moving. I slammed into him and his strong arms kept me from falling. My legs were shaking and I thought I might fall. They couldn't hold me up and we fell to the ground together, our arms wrapped around each other.

My hands shook as my fingers trembled on his face. His eyes watered and tears fell down his dirty, grimy face. Seth, my mind yelled because my voice didn't work.

He was alive.

He was here.

He was in my arms.

He ripped his gloves off and his hands were on my face as if he craved a skin-to-skin touch as much as I did. His fingers traced my cheeks, rubbed my lips. I grabbed his hands and he hissed and pulled back.

I reached for them again. I took them gently into my own. His right hand was mutilated, missing fingers, and covered in burn scars. My heart pounded in my chest. I couldn't imagine the pain, the suffering. My brain spun with not knowing what had happened.

Turning the hand over, I kissed the palm. He was here. He was alive. That was all that mattered. His other hand gripped my neck and he pulled me in for a real kiss. Lips to lips. Tongue to tongue. It started out tender and sweet, until our tears ran and covered our mouths with a salty taste. I wanted more. I wanted all of him.

A cough rumbled from the giant beside us. Large hands reached down and pulled us up. I craned my neck and looked up at him and shook my head.

"Teddy? Is that you?"

He enveloped me in a bear hug. "It sure is, Miss Emily."

"Miss Emily?" Seth repeated, pulling me back into his arms.

Teddy smiled. "This is the fine lady my boat is named after."

"You named your boat after me? That is so sweet."

I looked up at Seth and included the two others in their group. "Teddy was my husband's driver when we lived in San Francisco. He left when things started going bad so he could get back to his family."

"Your family?" I looked up at him, but Teddy just shook his head.

"I'm so sorry."

I turned in Seth's arms to acknowledge the others in his group. "Hello, I'm Emily."

The young woman smiled. "Oh, we figured that out already. All Seth has done is talk about Emily this and Emily that."

I blushed as she shook my hand.

"I'm Miranda and this is Cody," she said, hooking a thumb the young man's way. "I ran into Seth at the hospital after the attack and we picked up Cody at the library there in Concord, and you seem to know Teddy, the King of Pittsburg, already."

My head was spinning with all the adventures the group seemed to have had. I turned in Seth's arms and gave him another kiss. I knew I must have a stupid grin on my face, but I couldn't believe we'd found each other again. In a world without cell phones and computers, we'd managed to be in the same place at the same time. Only the cosmos could manage that. I said a prayer of thanks in my mind.

I introduced them to Nickie. Seth smiled at me at the canine's name and the dog jumped from person to person as if discovering new friends.

"I didn't name him. His nametag said he's called Nickie," I told Seth.

I turned to include everyone. "Let's get back to the new outpost and you can tell me all about what has happened on the way. The group relocated to an RV yard in Oakley. We're down to about twenty-five or so plus a group of kids who were there when the group arrived. You can tell me your stories first and then I'll tell you mine."

CHAPTER TWENTY-EIGHT

The walk back passed in a daze. I held Seth's hand and I didn't think I would ever let go. I'd cried with Seth when he told me of his mother's turning and how she'd attacked him. My heart broke as he explained he'd had to kill her. Tears ran down my face and the road was a blur as the young girl told me of sacrificing Seth's fingers to save his life. Would I have been brave enough to make that decision? If I had, would I have been able to do it?

I'd cried when Miranda told me of her time with Peters and escaping him, and I'd hugged her when she told me of being unable to kill him. I'd been terrified during my time with that evil man, and I hadn't suffered the abuse this young woman had. My free hand clenched into a fist. I'd been sure Antonio had killed him, although Miranda's description of what he had done to Peters was more than I could imagine that kind man I'd met doing. Okay, he'd invented the attack signal to use the zombies, so he wasn't all kind. But he'd been kind to me. The world wasn't what it had been. We were all being called upon to do the unspeakable just to survive.

I'd laughed at Cody telling of meeting Seth and Ran, as Seth called her, at the library, as much from the story as by his surfer-guy lingo. And I giggled when Teddy told me of his proclaiming himself King of Pittsburg. I smiled, imagining all too well this big man with the big heart declaring himself the ruler of all he surveyed. He'd always been meant for bigger things than driving and protecting Carl.

I left the recorder turned on, but I knew if the batteries failed, I had this group to cover my back. Having seen firsthand what the attack sound could do, they were amazed at what the repel portion could do.

"No one should be able to control the skinbags. It isn't right," Miranda said, with her face fierce and her eyes bright.

I watched as Cody wrapped himself around the young girl, but her eyes and Seth's met in a silent exchange. A twinge stung my heart that she'd been there for Seth and I hadn't. It passed as quick as it came. I had no room for jealousy of this brave young woman.

As we reached the sound barrier by the RV Park, I turned off the recorder. I grabbed Teddy's arm and whispered in his ear. He put his arms around the kids and scurried them along.

Seth turned to me, his eyes wary and alert.

"You didn't get to your telling of our time apart. Is there something you don't want the youngsters to know?" He nodded at the wall. "Or your friend Michelle who seems overexcited to see us. Does she know something I don't?"

He took a step back. "Do you have a new boyfriend or husband in there?"

The words I'd been about to say sputtered to a stop deep in my throat. How to begin?

"I lied to you."

"I knew it. You do still have a husband. Did he show up? You could have just said so. I would have understood. Everything is chaotic now. People disappear and show up out of the blue. We made no promises."

"Stop, just stop," I began, the words tumbling so fast so I wouldn't pause until I got it all out. "That isn't what I meant. I told you I couldn't have children. That it was safe to make love. But I guess I just couldn't have them with Carl. Because, I'm pregnant and you're the father and you don't have to do anything and I'm sorry and I didn't mean to trap you and I want this baby and I'm glad I'm having it."

"Are you done?" His voice was low and calm, too calm for my grocery-list of revelations.

"Yes," I said, staring at my dusty boots.

He grabbed my hands, pulled me to him, and swept me into his arms. He turned and faced the compound. Michelle and her gang of children lined the wall. Teddy, Miranda, and Cody waited at the gate.

"We are going to have a baby," Seth yelled at the top of his lungs.

Cheers erupted and I hid my heated face against his shoulder. I turned and looked into his eyes. His beautiful eyes filled with love and wet with unshed tears.

"Who would have thought?"

"Thought what?" I whispered.

"Who would have thought something as bad as the zombie apocalypse could bring me something as wonderful as Emily Gray?"

# # #

Dear Reader,

Love in the Time of Zombies is the book of my heart. It took three years to write in between my other projects. People ask me 'why zombies and romance?' I tell them, if someone can find romance with zombies out to eat you, limited resources, and renegades out to steal what you have, how hard can it be in real life? Go, get out there. Find your significant other. The zombie apocalypse could be right around the corner. You never know!

Thanks, Jill James

Author Note: To those readers familiar with the Brentwood, California area you may notice some anomalies. I used the area as it was in 2011 when I started the book, so all the wonderful improvements to my town didn't make it into the book.

Jill James didn't start out wanting to be a writer. She wanted to be a doctor, a lawyer, an astronaut, and President of the United States. Life happened and she realized she could be all of those things, in the pages of the books she wrote.

She lives in Nevada with her husband who is the inspiration behind all her romance novel heroes. When she isn't writing she is reading.

You can reach Jill online.
email: jill@jilljameswrites.com
Facebook: www.facebook.com/Jill.James.author
Twitter: www.twitter.com/jill_james

or drop a note.
Jill James
P.O. Box 61102
Reno NV 89506

Made in the USA
Middletown, DE
20 October 2021